MW01128215

BEST MAN
FOR HIRE

A FRONT AND CENTER STORY

TAWNA
FENSKE

This book is a work of fiction. Names, characters, places, and incidents are the product of the author's imagination or are used fictitiously. Any resemblance to actual events, locales, or persons, living or dead, is coincidental.

Copyright © 2014 by Tawna Fenkse. All rights reserved, including the right to reproduce, distribute, or transmit in any form or by any means. For information regarding subsidiary rights, please contact the Publisher.

Entangled Publishing, LLC
2614 South Timberline Road
Suite 109
Fort Collins, CO 80525
Visit our website at www.entangledpublishing.com.

Lovestruck is an imprint of Entangled Publishing, LLC.

Edited by Heather Howland
Cover design by Heather Howland
Cover art from DepositPhotos

Manufactured in the United States of America

First Edition December 2014

For my husband. Because I can actually call you that now, though you will always remain "my gentleman friend." Thank you, Craig, for being a daily source of support, laughter, inspiration, and all the things that make my toes curl.

Chapter One

Anna clicked her purple ballpoint pen and smiled at the couple twined together like sticky linguine on her office love seat. "So you want a fairy-tale wedding," she said.

It was a phrase uttered in the office of every wedding planner in America at least once a week. But at Anna's Wild Weddings in downtown Portland, Oregon, it meant something different.

"We're thinking *Little Red Riding Hood*," announced the bride, a twiggy blonde named Marci, who'd been referred to Wild Weddings by a couple whose frog-themed wedding Anna had orchestrated in August. "Darin already has his wolf costume from last Halloween, and my mother has this great vintage red cape, and the groomsmen can be woodsmen, and my grandmother can walk down the aisle carrying—"

Anna jotted brisk notes in her pink steno pad, pausing to murmur, "that sounds reasonable," or "how lovely" to requests she knew most wedding planners would deem neither reasonable nor lovely.

"And we want to include the phrase, 'all the better to eat you with, my dear' in the vows," the groom announced, giving his bride's knee a squeeze. "And maybe 'I'll huff, and I'll puff and I'll blow you—'"

"That one's actually *The Three Little Pigs*," Anna interjected. "Not that 'eat you' and 'blow you' aren't charming phrases to include in your nuptials. So do you have a date and place in mind?"

Marci nodded and caressed the groom's shoulder, her orange and blue-polka-dotted manicure clashing terribly with his green shirt. "Darin and I were thinking springtime in Hawaii," she said. "I know it's soon, but that's our favorite time of year there, and we want to do this before my grandmother is too feeble to travel."

"Hawaii?" Anna tapped her purple pen on her teeth and glanced at the calendar. "Any island in particular?"

Darin shrugged. "Not really. My family owns property on Maui, Kauai, and the Big Island, so any of those would work."

Anna glanced at the bride's handbag perched on the love seat beside her. A Louis Vuitton Alma Satchel, about eighteen hundred dollars, if Anna remembered right. Though they hadn't talked budget yet, Anna would bet her left butt cheek money was no object with this couple.

"Tell you what," Anna said. "I'm actually doing three other ceremonies on Kauai at the end of March. If you two wanted to aim for a few days on either side of that, I can cut you a deal on airfare for my assistant and me."

Darin perked up, solidifying Anna's theory that the wealthiest clients were always the ones most excited by a bargain. "We can do that," he said, beaming at his bride. "Right, honey?"

"Absolutely." Marci looked at Anna. "Just out of curiosity, what are the other weddings?"

Anna shrugged. "One nudist ceremony, one paintball wedding, and one totally normal ceremony."

"Normal?" Marci scrunched up her face in a way that reminded Anna of a first grader learning a new vocabulary word.

"Well, pretty normal," Anna amended. "The bride is a friend of a friend who comes from this big military family, and her overprotective brothers tricked her into hiring a Marine sniper as her nanny, but now she's marrying the manny and—"

"I like the sound of that paintball wedding," the groom interrupted, squeezing his bride's knee again. "The nudist one sounds cool, too. Maybe we could combine them?"

Marci frowned, clearly unwilling to give up her Red Ridding Hood dreams. "I don't know—"

"I don't advise it," Anna offered. "Those paintball weddings always turn vicious, and if you combine it with the nudist theme—well, you can imagine the welts."

Anna shot a pointed look at Darin's groin. His eyes widened. It was clear he didn't like imagining the welts. He gave an uncomfortable laugh and crossed his legs. "That sounds crazy anyway. People shouldn't do weird stuff like that for weddings."

"Totally," Marci agreed, beaming at Anna in silent thanks.

"Okay then," Anna said, clicking her purple pen. "How many axes will your woodsmen be needing?"

. . .

As soon as the happy couple linked arms and waltzed out the door—unlinking briefly when they got wedged in the doorframe—Anna kicked off her heels and grabbed her idea book. It was packed full of pictures and articles about weddings, and it never failed to get her brain simmering for the ones she was hired to plan.

She flipped the book open, her eyes falling on a photo of a tea-length white dress with beaded cap sleeves. A familiar lump lodged in her throat, but she swallowed it back and turned the page. An array of whimsical cake toppers lined up one row after another. One featured a bride pinching the groom's butt, while another had a groom dipping his bride midwaltz.

The lump fought its way back up her throat.

"The hell with you," Anna said, swallowing it back down as she tore her gaze from the book and fumbled for her phone. She hit the first speed dial number and waited for Janelle to pick up.

"Oh, thank God it's you!"

Anna smiled. "Because I'm your favorite sister in the whole world?"

"Absolutely," Janelle agreed, and Anna felt pleased at beating out the nonexistent competition. "Also, you're not Jacques. That's a definite mark in your favor."

"He's still calling?"

"All the time," Janelle said, her voice sounding more tired than Anna had heard it in a long time. "It's fine, I've got it under control. You didn't call to talk about my idiot ex, though. What's up?"

"I have a proposition for you."

"Does it involve cabana boys feeding me frozen grapes and giving me a pedicure?"

"Not quite, but close," Anna said, absently flipping the page on her wedding-idea book. "How would you feel about a free trip to Hawaii?"

"Hawaii?"

"I'm doing a bunch of destination weddings there back-to-back in March, and I need an assistant. I'll cover your airfare and hotel, of course."

"Which island? There's some pretty good shopping on Oahu."

"Not Oahu. Kauai, the garden island."

"The quiet one. I don't know, Anna. It's *Hawaii*."

She spoke the word the same way most women would say *prison* or *pap smear*.

"It's not prison, and it's not a pap smear," Anna said in case there was any confusion. "It's a warm, tropical place with palm trees and beaches and snorkeling."

"And bugs. And no subways. And hardly any people."

"That's part of the appeal. Well, maybe not the bugs." Anna flipped another page in her book, her fingers trailing over photos of colorful flower-girl dresses. "Come on, Janelle. You need the vacation, I need the help. Besides, you really ought to take a break from San Francisco. Get away from the city. Away from him."

"*Him*," Janelle repeated, sounding even less enthusiastic about Jacques than she had about Hawaii. "Do you really need the help, or are you being overprotective again?"

"If I admit it's a little of both, will that get you on the

plane?"

"No. But if one of my jobs can be sampling wedding cake, you've got yourself a deal."

Anna smiled, resting her palm on a photo of a bride carrying a shotgun adorned with pink camouflage for a hunting-themed wedding. "Come to Kauai and you can have all the wedding cake you want."

"Deal."

• • •

"Sheri says I need to pick a best man," Sam said.

Grant looked up from the beer bottle in his lap and regarded his soon-to-be brother-in-law with curiosity. "Didn't you say the twins are walking now? Have one of them do it."

"Charming as it might be to have to change the best man's diaper midceremony, there can only be one best man, and I'd rather not have to pick a favorite among my two new stepsons," Sam said. "The therapy could get expensive."

Grant grinned and propped his feet up on the railing of the tiny porch at the back of his small Kauai cottage. He'd bought the place years ago when PACOM first stationed him on Oahu. It was a quiet retreat when the Marines gave him leave, and a good source of rental income when they didn't.

He took a swig of beer and turned back to his fellow Marine and longtime pal. "So if it's not toddlers in tuxedoes, who'd you have in mind for a best man?"

Sam folded his arms over his chest and regarded Grant over the top of his sunglasses. "How about one of the bride's brothers? God knows she has enough of them, and you've been a pain in my ass for the better part of a decade."

Grant turned to the black-clad figure to his left and delivered a sturdy kick to Mac's shin. "Pay attention, MacArthur. One of us is getting drafted into service."

"What?" Mac looked up from his phone, and Grant wondered if his brother was plotting an arms deal or sexting his wife. Both required the same stoic concentration from Mac.

"A best man," Sam repeated, folding his arms over his chest and regarding his two future brothers-in-law with a look that made Grant want to jump off the balcony. "On one hand, Mac played a bigger role in fixing me up with Sheri."

Mac frowned. "I told you not to touch my sister, asshole."

Sam ignored Mac and turned back to Grant with a grin. "On the other hand, you and I served two tours together in Iraq. That counts for a helluva lot."

"Are you going to make us arm wrestle for this?" Grant asked, setting his beer down. "Because Mac cheats."

"I merely utilize superior tactical skills and strategic thinking," Mac retorted, picking up his beer.

"By punching me in the nuts?"

Mac shrugged and turned back to Sam. "Pick Grant. At the rate he's going, this is the closest he'll ever be to taking a walk down the aisle."

"Pick Mac," Grant argued back. "His quickie wedding on the beach in Mexico deprived him of a proper church ceremony of his own. You need to save his soul."

"Your souls are both beyond hope," Sam said. "Still, I'm glad you both made it here for the wedding."

"Wouldn't miss it for the world," Grant said, meaning it. "It was great of you guys to time it with my leave."

"You already reported to command in Honolulu?" Sam asked.

"Yeah. I've got a couple weeks to hang out here getting this place cleaned up and ready for some new renters, plus I volunteered to teach a self-defense class at the Women's Center."

Mac rolled his eyes and looked at Sam. "The disgusting thing? He's not even doing it to get laid."

Sam took a swig of his beer. "Come on, guys, focus. I need a best man. How about we do rock, paper, scissors for it?"

Mac shrugged, and Grant set his beer bottle down on the little table that separated his lounge chair from his brother's. "Works for me."

"Okay then," Sam said. "Ready?"

Both brothers put out a flat left palm. Sam nodded as Mac and Grant each balled up a right fist and began pounding it against the heel of their hand with more force than necessary.

"On three," Sam said. "One, two, *three*." He frowned. "What the hell is that?"

Mac held up his pointed index finger and thumb. "A pistol. A Browning 9-millimeter semiautomatic, to be precise."

"Ha!" Grant shouted, raising his fist with a thumb protruding. "Grenade beats pistol. I win, big brother."

Sam shook his head in disgust. "That doesn't count. Leave it to the Patton brothers to totally fuck up rock, paper, scissors."

Grant smiled and high-fived Mac. "I like to think we're improving it."

"You keep thinking that. It doesn't fucking count, and I still don't have a best man." Sam paused, frowning. "Has anyone heard from Schwartz?"

Grant felt all the air leave the room. He forced himself to keep a smile in place, but inside he wanted to curl up in a ball. Or punch something. Punching something would be more manly, definitely more fitting of a Patton.

Beside him, Mac grunted. "Ask numbnuts here. Grant's the only one who ever hears from him."

"He called Mom on her birthday," Grant protested, not sure why he felt the need to defend their reclusive brother. "And he sent a card when Sheri got engaged."

"No return address," Mac pointed out. "You're the only one who even knows where he lives."

"Must be a twin thing," Sam said. "Like when the boys decide to crap their pants at the same time."

"Exactly like that," Grant muttered, suddenly eager to escape. He picked up his beer bottle and stood, though he had no earthly idea where he planned to go. "We're Irish twins, remember? Eleven months apart."

Sam picked up his beer and took a slug. "You think Schwartz will make it to the wedding?"

Grant shook his head and walked over to the kitchen, his gaze landing on a framed photo from Mac's wedding. He and Sherri and Mac stood side by side on a beach in Mexico. Mac looked gruff and in love. Sheri looked windblown and beautiful. Grant looked cheerful, friendly, happy, and completely, utterly, full of shit.

Schwartz wasn't in the picture.

"No," Grant said, forcing his face into a neutral expression as he looked up from the photo and back to where the other men waited on the porch.

Even through Mac's dark sunglasses, Grant could feel his brother's gaze boring into him. He forced himself not to look away as he gripped the edge of the picture frame and ordered himself to keep breathing.

"How about a coin toss?" Sam suggested, clearing his throat. "For the best man gig?"

Grant swung his gaze to Sam and nodded. "Sure." He set the photo down and turned to the fridge. He grabbed two more beers, then trudged back to the porch, leaving the door open.

"A coin toss," Mac repeated, reaching up to grab the beer Grant offered him. "That's fair."

"Sure," Grant agreed, handing Sam the other beer. He leaned against the side of the house and folded his arms over his chest.

"Okay then," Sam said, fishing in the pocket of his shorts. "Heads or tails?"

Mac frowned. "What the hell kind of coin is that?"

"A foil-wrapped condom," Sam said, turning it over in his palm. "It's supposed to look like a coin. They handed them out at the bachelor party last night."

"That's disturbing on many levels," Mac said, taking a sip of his beer. "Not the least of which is that you're sleeping with our sister."

"I'm sleeping with my fiancée," Sam said, grinning. "She just happens to be your sister. Heads or tails, asshole?"

"Tails," Grant said, wanting to bring a quick end to the conversation. "Flip."

Sam tossed the condom in the air, and Grant watched it spin, thinking about love and loss and life and a lot of other things that were way to serious to ponder in the space of time it took a tacky prophylactic to arc its way back to his future brother-in-law's grip.

Sam clapped his hand over it the instant it landed. He drew his palm back and looked at Grant. "Tails it is. You're it, buddy. You're the best man."

"Fitting," Mac said, nodding over his beer. "You'll do us proud."

"I agree," Sam said, clapping Grant on the shoulder. "Between the brother who's a reclusive curmudgeon, the brother who's an overbearing control freak, and the brother who's a cheerful Boy Scout, I think I lucked out getting the Boy Scout."

Mac grunted and glanced down at his phone again. "I couldn't agree more."

"You guys are dicks," Grant said, pushing away from the wall. "But I'm honored anyway."

"You'll be a great best man," Sam said.

"The best," Mac agreed.

"I'm going for a walk," Grant said. "Try not to steal anything."

He headed for the front door, pausing just long enough to stuff his feet into a pair of tattered flip-flops before flinging the door open and escaping into the salt-scented breeze. He kept walking until he hit the beach, then kicked off the shoes beside a piece of driftwood. He spotted a broken bottle in the sand and nudged it next to his shoes so he'd remember to take it back with him to keep litter off the beach.

He stood up and hesitated a moment, then turned west and started walking. His pace was brisk, but he couldn't outrun his thoughts.

Best man? In what world could you possibly be the best man for anything?

Grant kicked his toes through the sand and began to run. The sea air felt good on his arms, and the sand was soft and warm underfoot. He passed a couple playing Frisbee near the water and offered them a friendly smile.

"Afternoon," he called. "Beautiful day."

"Sure is!"

He kept running, his pace strong and even. Rows of condos gave way to thick palms, and soon he'd lost sight of any other human life. This was his favorite part of this area of Kauai, his favorite spot on any of the Hawaiian Islands, really. It was possible to lose yourself completely.

Almost.

He'd been running at least thirty minutes when he spotted a cluster of people. Odd, considering few people even knew this section of beach even existed. The tourists sure as hell didn't know about it, and most locals stayed away on weekdays. He slowed his stride, frowning. Was he imagining things, or were all of them buck naked?

No, not all of them. His eyes landed on a woman in a bright yellow sundress. She had shoulder-length hair that glinted reddish-gold in the sun. As she turned toward him, her grass-green eyes lit up with something that looked like relief. Grant kept moving forward, almost without realizing his body was carrying him toward her.

For the first time in his life, Grant's brain tuned out the naked breasts around him and zeroed in on the one fully clothed woman in sight.

"Thank God you're finally here," she said, grabbing his arm.

Grant blinked at her, too stunned to reply.

Not that he had a chance to get a word out anyway. She kept talking, her words coming out in a jumbled rush.

"We were starting to get worried. Well, everyone except the rest of the groomsmen, who were all taking bets on whether the best man would make it, but now that you're here—"

"Best man," Grant repeated, his brain trying to wrap itself around her words.

"I don't mean to rush you, but you've got three minutes to take your clothes off and get oiled up," she said. "You can use that tent over there if you want, though I don't really see the point since you'll be running around naked for the next few hours."

He stared at her. He knew it wasn't polite, but it was hard not to admire the lush curve of her breasts beneath the yellow sundress, and the taut muscles in her calves. Her toes were bare and tipped with bright orange polish, and the inside of her right ankle bore a small tattoo of a feather. Her arms were long and pale, but shapely. He looked back up at her face, which was framed by straight, shoulder-length hair the color of carrot cake.

She frowned at him and spit out a lock of it, and Grant wondered if it tasted like cinnamon and nutmeg. He was thinking of running his fingers through it when a gust of wind blew her hair across her face, showing two bright blue streaks mixed in with the auburn strands.

Interesting.

The woman tightened her grip on his arm, and Grant lost his breath for an instant.

"Come on, buddy," she said. "We've been waiting on you. Off with the clothes already."

Another woman joined them, wearing nothing but a short veil and pair of sunglasses. She touched the redhead's arm and leaned close. "Actually, Anna, this isn't—"

"Sure I am," Grant said, and reached for the hem of his shirt.

Chapter Two

"You're not the best man," Anna said flatly, trying to keep her cheeks from flaming, her voice from shaking, and her eyes from drifting to anything that would make either task harder.

Harder.

"Well, that all depends," he said, smiling down at her in a way that made her insides turn molten. "Whose wedding are we talking about here?"

"Th—this wedding," she stammered, swallowing hard. "The one right now."

"This is a wedding?" He pulled his gaze from hers and surveyed the scene around them. Anna swallowed hard, trying to imagine how it looked to his eyes.

His eyes.

God, they were the most remarkable shade of blue gray, almost like the ocean on a stormy morning.

And at the moment, they were taking in the sight of four

naked bridesmaids playing Frisbee with three equally naked groomsmen. Anna swallowed and tried to pull his attention back to the matter at hand.

"So if you're not the best man, why do you have your shirt off?"

He looked back at her and gave a halfhearted shrug, while Anna did her very best not to notice the ripple of muscle in his broad shoulders. His left biceps bore a tattoo of some sort of military insignia, and Anna squinted for a better look.

"You told me to take off my shirt," he pointed out as he reached for his belt buckle. "My pants, too, if I recall. Just following orders."

His eyes glittered with laughter Anna could tell he was working to contain. She wondered what it would be like to tickle him until he gave up and burst out laughing. Before she knew it, she was imagining her fingers stroking those hard, glorious abs as she twined her nails in that dark chest hair and rubbed her—

"I see," Anna said, taking a step back. "That is, I'm seeing a whole lot more of you than I probably should. I'm very sorry for the confusion, Mr.—"

"Patton. Grant Patton. You can call me Grant."

"Grant Patton?" She blinked. "*The* Grant Patton?"

"I'm not sure I require a definite article before my name, but yeah. Do we know each other?"

"You're the photographer," she blurted, feeling foolish. "I saw your photos. The engagement photos you took for Mac and Kelli? They were incredible. I've been planning weddings for more than ten years, and those were the best images I've ever seen. You're Mac's brother?"

He nodded and regarded her with renewed curiosity. "And you're Kelli's friend the wedding planner? Funny we never crossed paths in Mexico."

"Right. Well, after Mac and Kelli decided on a simple little family-only ceremony on the beach, and I had to hurry home for another wedding I was organizing and—wait, you're here in Hawaii for Sheri's wedding?"

"Yep. She was kind enough to time it with my leave. I'm the best man." He grimaced, and Anna wondered what that was about.

"Okay, well, I'm really very sorry about all this."

"I'm not," he said, holding her gaze. "Not at all."

Anna swallowed and turned away. As if on cue, a wiry man with gray hair and a long beard came dashing down the beach, throwing clothes off as he ran. "Sorry I'm late, guys! You haven't started yet?"

"*This* is the best man," the bride said to Anna, grabbing the newcomer by the arm. "Bob, this is Anna Keebler, the wedding planner. This is—I'm sorry, what was your name again?"

"Grant Patton."

"Well, Grant, you're welcome to stick around for the ceremony if you like, but you'll have to be nude," the bride said. "This is a nude wedding, so only the staff can wear clothing. Well, except me." She grinned and touched the edge of her veil. "Anna insisted I could still wear this."

"It's a mantilla veil with lace edging," Anna said, turning to adjust the comb. "My absolute favorite veil I've ever seen on a bride. Worth making an exception."

She saw Grant smiling from the corner of her eye, and she turned to see him watching her instead of the bride's bare breasts.

A gentleman.

"I appreciate the offer to stick around, but I have to run," he said. "I'll be seeing you around though, Anna."

"Oh?" She swallowed, wondering if he was asking her out.

"The wedding. Sam and Sheri?"

"Sam and Sheri, right, of course. Absolutely. It's going to be a wonderful ceremony."

"I'm sure it is." He held her gaze a few more beats, then nodded. "Nice meeting you."

He slung his T-shirt around his shoulders and turned away. He began to jog back the direction he'd come, muscles rippling in the sunlight. His calves were strong and lean, and his bare back glistened with sweat, and Anna pictured him in the shower after a long run, water sluicing over his bronze skin, those massive hands rubbing soap over his chest, then lower until his fingers slid around—

"Who was *that*?"

Anna turned to see her sister moving toward her along the beach. She wore a green dress and an expression of utter amazement.

"Grant Patton," Anna said, savoring the taste of his name on her tongue. "He's the brother of the bride in the final wedding we're doing."

"How do you know him?"

"I don't. Not at all. But he took the most amazing engagement photos for my friend, Kelli, in Mexico."

"He's a photographer?"

"I don't think that's his job. I'm pretty sure he's a military guy of some sort. Marines, maybe."

"That explains why he's built like a tank. You should ask him out. You could use a vacation fling."

"Please," Anna said, feeling the heat creep into her cheeks. "He's hardly my type."

Janelle rolled her eyes. "That's right, you like narcissistic, tortured artist types who won't commit."

"Not true." Anna bit her lip, knowing it was completely true.

Not that Janelle knew the reason.

"He doesn't need to be your type for a fling," Janelle pointed out. "He looks like he'd be great in bed."

"Janelle!"

"Well he does."

"I'm here in a professional capacity organizing a wedding for his sister. A fling would not be a smart move."

Janelle shrugged. "Fine." She was quiet a moment, and Anna let her gaze wander down the beach to where the bride and groom were taking turns swatting each other with palm fronds while the photographer clicked away with his camera. She'd had to pay Bryce extra to agree to work a nude wedding, something he felt compromised his artistic integrity.

"I talked to Jacques," Janelle blurted.

Anna gritted her teeth and turned back to her sister. "Why are you calling your ex-husband?"

"I didn't say *I* called *him*."

"You didn't have to. I know you. You're here in Hawaii, feeling nostalgic about your wedding, wondering how he's doing, so you pick up the phone—"

"She's pregnant," Janelle said. "His girlfriend's pregnant."

Anna winced and squeezed her sister's hand. "I'm sorry."

Janelle sighed and shook her head. "It is what it is."

"Which is a giant clusterfuck of a marriage that ended when your ex turned into a psycho control freak who couldn't keep his dick in his pants." Anna meant to keep the venom out of her voice, but it didn't quite work out. Truth be told, she was probably angrier at herself than she was at Jacques, but her sister didn't need to know that.

"Anyway," Janelle said. "He claims it doesn't mean anything. That he still wants me back."

"I hope you told him to go fuck himself."

"With a flaming potato."

"Good girl." Anna sighed. "I'm so sorry, hon."

"Quit saying that," Janelle said. "I don't want us to be sorry. I want us to be wild and carefree and happy and maybe a little bit drunk for the next few days. I want us to have crazy flings with inappropriate men and go home with sand wedged in uncomfortable body crevices."

"Thank you for that mental picture," Anna said. "You do remember we're here to work, right?"

"Of course." Janelle looked back at the bride and groom. "Speaking of which, I should probably go spray the wedding party with more sunscreen."

"Watch out for the groomsman with the goatee. He's very handsy."

"I noticed."

"The bride and groom look happy though."

Anna watched the groom trying to juggle a trio of coconuts and tried not to notice which parts of him looked happiest. The bride stood nearby, watching her husband-to-be with a disturbing mix of admiration and lust.

"So you're really never going to do it?"

Anna snapped her attention off the groom's anatomy

and looked at her sister. "Do it?"

"Get married. I can't believe you plan weddings for a living and you never want to get married."

Anna shrugged. "I love weddings, but marriage isn't really my thing."

"I know, you've been saying that for years, but I figured you'd change your mind."

"About getting married?" Anna shook her head, fighting to keep her voice bright and even. "Definitely not. Marriage holds zero appeal for me. Besides, I'm much too busy."

Janelle folded her arms over her chest and frowned. "Too busy to be married? You're aware this isn't 1946, right? Women don't get married and stay home milking cows and doing laundry by hand in a washtub."

"Cows and laundry have nothing to do with why I don't want to get married."

"So what is it then?"

Anna shook her head and turned away. She'd never shared the secret with her sister, and she wasn't about to do it now. She rummaged in the woven tote she'd parked next to a piece of driftwood and came up with a can of spray sunscreen.

"Here," she said, thrusting it into Janelle's hands. "Go make sure the groom doesn't sunburn anything he's going to need for the honeymoon. I'll go do the rest of the wedding party."

"Fine. But don't think I didn't notice you're avoiding the question."

"I wouldn't dream of it," she said, and went off to spray SPF on strangers' bare butts.

. . .

The next morning, Grant was dozing under a tree beside the Wailua River. Though he held a fishing pole in one hand, it was unlikely he'd catch any fish. There was no hook on the end of his line.

He yawned and tipped his hat over his face, shading himself from the early morning sun. The earthy scent of river water hung in the air as water lapped at the red-dirt shore and a family of chickens clucked cheerfully in a near-by shrub.

Grant stretched his legs out in front of his sand chair. They were still a little stiff from yesterday's unexpected jog on the beach, which served him right. Running off like some kind of lunatic to avoid awkward family conversations was probably not the best way to deal with things.

Still, the beautiful woman on the beach had been a nice surprise. *Anna.* He combed his memory for any details he could recall about her. Mac's wife, Kelli, had roomed with her in college for a while. He knew she lived in Portland and owned a wedding-planning business, and he knew his sister had hired her on Kelli's recommendation. Those facts he'd filed in the back of his brain the same way he'd cataloged a grocery list or the names of the players on the Seattle Mariners baseball team.

But now that he'd met her in real life, something felt different. Every detail about her seemed like a valuable gem, worth turning over in his palm and studying in a different light. He was intrigued by the bright flashes of color in her hair—the natural hue of carrot cake mixed with the subtle blue just behind her ear. He remembered the feather tattoo on the inside of her right ankle and wondered what the significance was. Did she have a boyfriend? Husband? He hadn't seen a wedding ring, but maybe she didn't wear one. She certainly seemed a little unconventional.

Grant wasn't sure when he nodded off or how long he'd been out. All he knew was that a woman's scream jarred him awake with his heart thudding in his ears. He jumped to his feet and surveyed his surroundings, years of military training commanding him to identify the threat.

The woman screamed again, and Grant whirled around.

There was Anna, standing in the water with blood pouring down her chest.

On the shore, a man leveled a gun at her and fired.

Chapter Three

Anna had no idea where Grant came from.

One minute she was ordering Janelle to stop squealing like a four-year-old every time Bryce the photographer fired the paintball gun.

The next thing she knew, Bryce was flat on his back with Grant's massive forearm across his windpipe.

Anna gulped and splashed out of the water, her bare feet slipping on the soggy red earth.

"Grant!" she yelled, before it occurred to her she should probably be yelling Bryce's name. He was the one flailing with Grant's knee to his groin.

Grant looked up just as Anna reached his side. Janelle was three steps behind, panting for breath.

"Stop, Grant!" Anna gasped. "What are you doing?"

"Urg," said Bryce.

Grant released the pressure on Bryce's throat, but kept him pinned to the ground. He turned and stared at Anna's chest. "You're bleeding."

Alarmed, she looked down at herself. With a flutter of relief, she swiped a hand over her breastbone and held it out for him to see. "It's paint. Red paint, I swear. Nontoxic, water-based paint so it doesn't hurt the fish."

Grant blinked, but didn't move. "But you screamed. And the gun—"

"A paintball gun," Janelle said, toeing it with her bare foot. It had come to rest about three feet out of Bryce's reach, which Anna thought was probably a good thing.

"It was Janelle screaming," Anna said. "She doesn't like guns, even paintball guns."

Janelle folded her arms over her chest. "Not when they're aimed at my sister."

"It's practice for a wedding," Anna said. "A paintball wedding later this week. Bryce is the photographer, and he wanted to make sure—"

"A paintball wedding," Grant repeated.

"Yes," Anna said. She watched him process the information and couldn't help noticing his eyes again. The hue was like no eye color she'd seen before. The gray was warm, almost taupe, which sounded ridiculous when she thought of it that way, but it looked great on him.

Grant looked down at Bryce, who still hadn't spoken. "And you're the photographer?"

The man tried to draw himself up into a sitting position, which was impossible with Grant's elbow wedged into his chest. Grant shifted his weight, making it easier for Bryce to breathe, but not much else.

"I'm *not* the photographer anymore!" Bryce huffed. "They flew me out here to photograph all these ridiculous weddings, and it's been one atrocity after another. First the bride and groom want me to shoot from the water where there are *sharks*—"

"It's a river," Anna pointed out. "There are no sharks."

"—and then another pair of lunatics expects me to go traipsing through the jungle with poisonous snakes—"

"It's Hawaii," Anna said. "There are no snakes."

"—and now I've been *assaulted*," Bryce spat, glaring up at Grant. "I've had it with this place. I'm catching the first flight back to the mainland. You can find another damn photographer."

He squirmed and struggled and flailed until Grant pressed a palm to his chest and held him still. Grant looked up at Anna. "You want me to let him go?"

Anna shrugged. "I can't exactly hold him hostage and force him to take pictures."

Grant looked back at him. "I could probably arrange for the hostage thing."

She shook her head, though she didn't doubt he was capable of it. "It's fine, let him go."

"You're free, Bryce," Grant said, releasing the indignant photographer from his grip. Grant stood and offered a hand up. "I'm very sorry about the misunderstanding."

Bryce stared at the proffered hand like Grant had just blown his nose in it. He sputtered with disgust and struggled to his feet without assistance. Anna reached out and began dusting red dirt off his sleeves, but Bryce slapped her hand away.

She winced and drew back. Grant took a step toward Bryce, his eyes glittering with fury. Anna put her hand on Grant's arm and shook her head. "It's okay."

"It is *not* okay," Bryce snapped. "You'll be hearing from my lawyer about this."

He turned and stomped away.

They all watched him go, politely restraining their laughter when Bryce tripped on a vine and shrieked, "Snake!" before kicking it into the grass.

For a brief moment, Anna considered going after him. Three of her four wedding couples *had* requested Bryce out of all the photographers Anna worked with. She'd paid to fly him out here, and the couples had paid hefty deposits.

Before Anna could take a step forward, Bryce turned, flipped them off, and flung open the door to his rental car.

Anna sighed. "Have a safe trip," she called.

"Bite me!" Bryce yelled and revved the engine.

The second his car was out of sight, Grant shook his head. He turned to Anna, looking like a dog that had just chewed up the newspaper. "I'm really very sorry," he said. "I didn't mean to ruin anyone's wedding."

"You didn't ruin any weddings," Anna assured him, though that remained to be seen. Now what was she going to do? But Grant looked guilty, so she added, "I can see why you might have assumed we needed help."

"Though we're unaccustomed to defining *help* as a chokehold," Janelle added.

"I shouldn't have been so rough," Grant insisted.

"There's a time and a place for roughness," Anna assured him, flushing when she realized how that sounded. Grant looked like the sort of guy who knew all about a time and a place for roughness. "Your instincts were good, even if the situation didn't call for that."

Janelle grinned and gave Grant a nudge with her elbow.

"So, tough guy—know any photographers we could get on short notice?"

Grant scratched his chin, considering. "Well, there's Pete Nicholson over on the north shore but he usually books up months in advance. Probably the same with Katie Kurtail from Dream Images, or—"

"She's talking about you," Anna interrupted. "That was Janelle's idea of a subtle hint."

"Me?"

"I told her about the engagement photos you took for Mac and Kelli."

Janelle nodded, eyeing Grant up and down, and Anna resisted the urge to yank her sister's ponytail. "She said you've got a great eye."

"He does have great eyes." Anna coughed. "I mean a great eye. For photography. But I'm not sure this is a good idea."

"Why not?" Janelle asked.

"Well, for starters, he's not a wedding photographer."

"But you said yourself he took the best engagement photos you've ever seen. Weren't they even on a beach?"

"Yes, but besides that, we don't even know he's available or what his fees are like."

Janelle rolled her eyes. "We could ask him instead of standing here talking about him like he doesn't speak English."

Grant shook his head. "Your sister's right," he told Janelle. "I'm not really a wedding photographer. That was just a one-time thing."

"One-time things can sometimes turn into more," Janelle argued.

"It was a photo shoot, Janelle, not a one-night stand in a romantic comedy," Anna said. "Wedding photography is a very specialized art. We don't even know if Grant has the skill do it."

She didn't mean for it to sound like a challenge, but the flash in Grant's eyes told her he'd taken it as one. He folded his arms over his chest and leveled his gaze at her.

"I said I wasn't a wedding photographer, not that I couldn't do it," he said. "I minored in photography in college, and I've kept my skills sharp shooting for friends and freelance gigs over the years. I've had several special assignments from the Department of Defense to photograph combat zones for military public affairs. I'm not exactly a photographic novice here."

"With all due respect," Anna said, "shooting pictures of hand grenades is a little different from shooting pictures of brides."

"Both sound volatile, deadly, and likely to explode at a moment's notice."

"I can't argue with that." Anna bit her lip, considering her options. Finding a photographer on short notice on a small island would be next to impossible. She could try to talk Bryce into coming back, but she knew from experience that wasn't likely. Besides being temperamental and moody, he was stubborn as hell. She sighed and considered the hulking Marine in front of her.

"Would you even want the assignment? You'd be paid, of course, but still."

"I don't need the money."

She raised an eyebrow at him. "What would you do it for then?"

"Because I'm a nice guy." He almost sounded glum about that.

"Do you have a portfolio?" she asked. "Something I could look at, maybe show to all the other couples so they can decide if they want to use you?"

"Nothing formal, but I could walk you through a few of the photo collections on my computer. How about tonight at my place?"

Anna felt her mouth go dry and she licked her lips. "Your place?"

"Sure. I'll even make dinner. Come over early, maybe five?"

"I—well, I—"

"She'd love to," Janelle said, giving Anna a small shove. "Here, write your address down on this."

Before Anna could protest, her sister was handing him a small notepad and pen. Anna just stood there like an idiot, trying to think of something to say that didn't involve blurting out a desire to see him shirtless again. Grant took the notebook and flipped to a blank page. His writing was neat and clear, each number in perfect form even though the page didn't have lines.

"Here you go," he said, handing her the notepad. "See you at five."

"Five it is." Anna reached out to shake his hand, expecting a dry, professional grasp in return.

There wasn't anything unprofessional in the way Grant took her hand, but something in his touch sent a jolt of electricity buzzing through Anna's fingertips and all the way up her arm. His palm was huge and warm, and the strength in his fingers prompted several parts of her body to stand up and request site visits.

Part of her wanted to draw her hand back.

Most of her wanted to grab his other hand and put it on her butt.

Anna met his eyes and saw his expression was warm, but serious. His fingers gripped hers with a fierceness that surprised her.

"Just so you know," he said, "I don't generally condone violence."

"Aren't you a Marine?"

"I specialize in counterintelligence and human intelligence."

"What does that mean?"

"I catch spies, or I get other people to catch spies. I don't kill them. Much."

"That's reassuring."

"Anyway, I really am sorry about Bryce."

Anna nodded and bit the inside of her lip. "Thank you. I'm not sure I'm that sorry."

"Me neither. I was being polite."

"We try not to make that a habit around here," Janelle said.

Grant smiled and drew Anna's hand to his lips. She shivered as he planted a chaste kiss across her knuckles.

"See you tonight, Anna."

She watched him go, her heart lodged thickly in her throat. Her hand was still tingling long after he was out of sight.

• • •

"So let me get this straight," Mac said as he handed Grant a bottle of wine. "You're making dinner for a woman you don't know to land a photography job you don't want for a paycheck you refuse to accept."

Grant set the wine on the counter and got to work hunting for the meat mallet, ignoring his brother's look of dismay. "I didn't say I didn't want the job. Just that wedding photography isn't really my thing."

"And neither is wine. You want a corkscrew for that, not a hammer."

"What would I do without you, big brother?" Grant began unwrapping the butcher paper from two steaks he'd grabbed earlier at the grocery store. He laid them on the cutting board, arranging them carefully with their edges touching. He sprinkled each one with a healthy dusting of salt and pepper, doing his best to ignore Mac's gaze following his every move. He wiped his hands on a paper towel, then picked up the mallet. "The photo shoot sounds interesting, and the girls need help," he said. "I'm doing it as a favor."

He could feel his brother studying him, but he refused to make eye contact. Instead, he focused on pounding the holy hell out of the steak. Mac was silent, watching. Grant drew his arm back and smacked the meat harder, the one-pound mallet solid in his hand.

"Are you tenderizing that meat or punishing it?"

Grant gave it one more whack and set the mallet down. He moved to the sink to wash his hands. "Don't you ever feel like doing something for a stranger just to be nice?"

"No."

"Well I do."

"Clearly. I imagine it doesn't hurt that Anna is quite

attractive."

Grant gave a grunt of acknowledgment, but refused to offer more. Instead, he yanked a knife out of the block and grabbed one of the russet potatoes he'd washed earlier. He pulled out a clean cutting board and set the potatoes in the middle. Drawing the knife back, he eyed his target. He stabbed a small, clean hole right in the center of the first potato. He studied it, then drew the knife back again. Only a hole or two was really necessary to keep it from exploding when he baked it, but a few more wouldn't hurt.

Grant stabbed the potato a few more times, then reached for the second one.

"For a chronically nice guy, you have serious aggression issues in the kitchen," Mac said, shaking his head in Grant's peripheral vision. "So this photo gig—are you doing this to get laid, or because you can't resist the urge to do favors for people?"

The knife slipped in midstab, and Grant nearly took his thumb off. Good thing for quick reflexes. He set the knife down and reached into the drawer beside him for the foil.

"I'm just trying to help out," he said, maneuvering past his brother. "I'm the one who screwed things up, so I'm trying to make it right."

"Are we still talking about tackling the wedding photographer?"

Grant felt his gut twist, but he ignored it and grabbed the first potato. "What the hell else would we be talking about?"

Grant didn't answer, and Mac said nothing else. When he finally stole a look at his brother, Mac was watching him with his usual unreadable expression.

How much does he know?

Grant cleared his throat. "I need to grab the foil out of that cupboard."

Mac stepped aside, folding his arms over his chest as he leaned against the fridge. "Don't forget you're going to need to come up with a best man toast for Sheri's wedding."

Grant groaned inwardly. "Yeah, about the best man thing. I'm really not sure I'm best man material."

Mac gave a snort of disgust. "What the hell are you talking about?"

"I'm sure there's someone else more qualified—"

"Don't give me that bullshit. You're the best man to be the best man."

"I don't think—"

"You're doing it. You'll be the goddamn best man if I have to tie you up and drag you there myself."

"That'll look good in pictures."

Grant knew it was futile to keep arguing, so he didn't bother. He finished wrapping up the potatoes and walked outside to shove them in the coals on his grill. He poked them around a little, making sure they were situated just right.

When he came back in, Mac was still leaning against the fridge. "Thank you for grabbing the wine," Grant said. "I didn't have the first clue what went with steak. What do I owe you?"

"The promise that you'll quit being a jackass about the best man gig. And stop maiming perfectly good groceries."

Mac looked like such a hard-ass standing there with his arms crossed and his dark glasses shielding his eyes from the glare of the kitchen, and Grant started to laugh in spite of himself.

"Fine," he said. "Now get out. Anna's going to be here any minute."

As if on cue, the doorbell chimed. Before Grant could run to answer it, Mac was striding to the front room. He got to the door first, yanking it open while Grant was still three paces behind.

"Anna," Mac said, waving her inside like a perfect god-damn gentleman while Grant just stood there like an idiot staring at her. She wore a pale blue dress that brought out the subtle blue streaks nearly hidden in the bright strands of coppery hair. She tucked a swath of it behind her ear and smiled at him, and Grant felt his heart smack hard against his ribs.

"Hello," was all he could manage.

"Hi," she murmured, looking from him to Mac and back again.

"Good to see you again, Anna," Mac said. "It appears you've finally met the nice Patton brother."

Anna laughed and stepped inside, holding out a bottle of wine that looked a lot different than what Mac had brought. Did white wine go with steak? Grant stepped forward to take the bottle, his hand brushing hers and sending a warm pulse of energy through his hand. Anna smiled again, then turned back to Mac.

"If Grant's the nice brother, what does that make you?"

"I'll leave it to my wife to answer that one," Mac answered, "but I suspect she'd say I'm the scary brother."

She cocked her head to the side and turned to study Grant, her eyes flashing over him so thoroughly he wondered if she could see right through his clothes. The thought made him a little dizzy, and also made him wonder what she was wearing under that flowery blue sundress. The straps were skinny, so she couldn't be wearing a bra, could she? Her feet were bare, but he could see flip-flops poking out of the top of her purse. The feather tattoo on her ankle looked delicate and lovely, and Grant felt himself sigh inwardly.

"The scary brother, huh?" she said, raising an eyebrow at Mac before meeting Grant's eyes again. "From what little I know of Grant, I'd say he has plenty of scary of his own. He just hides it better."

Mac stared at her a few beats, then nodded. "An astute observation." He turned and looked at Grant. "Now if you'll excuse me, my wife is expecting me."

"Give her a kiss for me," Anna said.

"Preferably one without too much tongue," Grant added.

Mac nodded to Anna, then Grant, then strode out the door and into the bright sunlight. Grant watched him move toward the drivers' side door of his black Town Car, his dark hair gleaming in the sun. Grant shook his head, then shut the door and turned back to Anna.

He smiled, feeling a funny flutter in his gut at the prospect of being alone with her. "Welcome," he said, hefting the wine. "Thank you for bringing this. Can I get you a glass?"

"I prefer to drink straight from the bottle."

"In that case, I can wrap it up in a paper bag for you to keep things classy."

She grinned. "I'll have a glass of wine in a few minutes." She set her tote bag on the floor and stepped into the middle of the living room, turning in a full circle to take in all angles of the little cottage. He tried to imagine how she saw it, all rustic wood furniture and pale turquoise paint with white trim. He'd worked hard to make it homey, the perfect retreat.

Anna completed her circle and met his eyes again. "Wow, this place is adorable. You own it?"

He nodded. "I had three back-to-back tours in Iraq. Took my combat pay and bought this place a couple years ago when the recession made property a little more afford-able in Kauai."

"Don't you worry about someone breaking in when you're overseas?"

"Nah, my brother does private security. He set me up with a system that would stop a Viking invasion."

The second the words left his mouth, he knew what was coming. He watched her face register surprise and knew the question she'd ask before those gorgeous lips formed the words. "Mac does private security?"

"Not Mac. Schwartz. Another brother. He's…not around very much."

Her gaze held his a few beats longer than comfortable, and Grant fought not to look away. Instead, he held eye con-tact and took a step closer, moving deliberately into her per-sonal space. "You live in Portland, right?"

She blinked, then nodded. "That's right. Moved there from San Francisco for college and never went back. My sis-ter—you met Janelle—she stayed in the city."

He gave her his best Boy Scout smile and nodded, putting his active listening skills to use. "You like it in Portland?"

"Very much. That's where I met Mac's wife, Kelli. We roomed together for a while."

"But your sister likes it better in San Francisco?"

Anna nodded, not moving back, but clearly affected by his nearness. Was it the normal result of Grant's subtle inter-rogation tactics, or something more?

"She's a city girl at heart," Anna said, her voice a little faint. Grant watched her throat move as she swallowed, and he wondered what it would feel like to plant a trail of kisses from under her chin all the way to her collarbone. "Even Portland's too small for her."

"The two of you are close?"

"Very." She smiled, an expression that lit up her whole face and almost swayed Grant from what he was aiming for, which was to keep her talking so she wouldn't feel the need to ask him too many questions. She smoothed her hand over the back of his overstuffed easy chair and shrugged. "I'm sure Janelle would tell you I'm a bit smothery and overbearing, but that's what older siblings are for, right?"

Grant thought about Mac and nodded, but didn't add anything. He waited for her to fill the silence, to keep talking so he wouldn't have to.

She shrugged again and kept going, which gave Grant a chance to study the side of her face. She had beautiful cheekbones, and the coppery hue of her hair made her green eyes flash with color.

"Our parents divorced when I was eight and Janelle was six, and I guess that bonded us in a weird way," she continued, stepping away from him just a little. "I sort of felt responsible for her, you know?"

Grant nodded, holding her gaze with his. "That must have been hard."

"It is. *Was*." She gave a funny little laugh and swallowed hard—a telltale sign the subject made her nervous—and looked down at her hands on the back of the chair. "Geez, listen to me. I'm almost thirty and I'm prattling on about my parents' divorce like some sort of heartbroken adolescent. I don't usually do this."

He felt a small pang of guilt then, but what the hell else was he supposed to do? He needed to control the situation. He needed to be the one asking questions. If she kept sharing, he didn't have to. It was as simple as that.

"Would you like to see the rest of the house?" he asked. "It's pretty small, but I did most of the renovations myself."

"I'd love to."

"You sure I can't get you a glass of wine?"

She seemed to hesitate, then shrugged. "Sure, why not."

"Red or white?"

"White."

"Assuming you don't really want to drink from the bottle, do you want a stemless wineglass or one with a stem?"

"Doesn't matter. God, you really are the perfect host."

He shook his head. "Not really. My sister gave me the glasses because she was tired of drinking out of mason jars when she visited. You brought the white; Mac brought the red. All I'm doing is uncorking it."

"Honest, too. *And* you cook. What else are you perfect at?"

Her cheeks went pink the instant she spoke the words, and Grant had to stop himself from lunging for her mouth. He should be a gentleman here.

"Stick around and find out."

Okay, he wasn't that much of a gentleman. Anna blinked in response, then smiled. "You plan to show me something besides your photos?"

"I'll show you anything you ask to see." He cleared his throat and gestured toward the next room. "But first, let's start with the house." He set the wine bottle on the counter and pulled out a corkscrew. Yanking the cork out with a firm tug, he grabbed a glass from the rack beside the sink and splashed a little wine into it.

Handing her the glass, he moved past her down the hall. He felt her fall into step behind him, and he continued down the narrow hallway until he reached the center. He turned a bit too abruptly, and she collided with his chest.

"Sorry about that," he said.

"Not a problem." She touched her hand to his chest, and he watched in pleasured fascination as she stroked her fingertips over the space between his pecs. He wondered if she could feel how hard his heart was pounding. She dropped her hand and took a step back.

"Sorry, I splashed a little wine on you. Just getting it off."

"Getting it off. Good." Grant cleared his throat. "Right here is the office, which doubles as a guest room when I have company. There's the guest bath, which I added on just after I bought the place. Master bedroom is down there." He waved faintly in that direction, not wanting to seem too lecherous or threatening by stalking her through his bedroom just minutes after she'd arrived. She stepped past him, walking into the room by herself. Grant trailed behind, trying not to get too close.

"This headboard is incredible," she said, moving closer to his bed and bending over with her hands planted on the mattress. Grant stared at her ass and felt himself go dizzy. She was just peering at the woodwork, for chrissakes. It wasn't an invitation, not even when she turned to look at him over her shoulder. "Where did you find it?"

"I built it," he said, not sure if the clench in his gut was pride or a fervent desire to lift up her dress and take her from behind. "I do a little woodworking as a hobby."

"A hobby?" She ran her fingers over the intricate carvings in the wood and shook her head. "A hobby is knitting scarves or playing chess. This is masterful. You really made this? It looks like the bench in the lobby at the National Tropical Botanical Gardens. We were there this morning scouting for another wedding."

"Yeah, I carved that, too," he said, and watched her jaw drop. "I donated it last spring. Some charity thing they were doing."

"Okay, now you're just ridiculous." She shook her head and took a sip of wine. "Please tell me you've got some sort of hideous fault. A huge goiter or a habit of tripping preschoolers in the mall?"

He laughed and shook his head. "Come on. Let's get going on dinner."

He led her back down the hallway, through the kitchen, and out to the patio, where he pulled out an Adirondack chair for her and dusted the seat off with his hand. "Have a seat while I get the grill fired up. How do you like your steak?"

"Medium rare. Is there something I can do to help?"

"Nope, already under control. I made my mom's famous coleslaw a couple hours ago, and the potatoes have been in here for a while. More wine?"

"I'm good for now, thanks."

Grant gave the coals a few fierce stabs with a poker, then set the meat on the grill, fanning the smoke away from his face. "So how did you get to be a wedding planner?"

"I got my degree in business and started out working for a normal wedding planner. Then I realized there was an unfilled need for someone specializing in nontraditional weddings."

"Nontraditional?"

"Offbeat. Women who want a ceremony where everyone dresses up in steampunk costumes, or guys who've always dreamed of a pirate-themed wedding on a ship. I help make their dreams a reality."

"And what about your dreams?" he asked, shutting the lid of the grill to trap the heat as he turned and looked at her again. "I assume a wedding planner has pretty definite ideas about her own eventual wedding?"

Anna shook her head and took a sip of wine. "Nope."

"No ideas?"

"No wedding. Not something I want to do."

"Ever?"

"Never," she said, nodding a little as she said it, which was an odd gesture. People who nodded while denying something were usually lying, in Grant's experience. It was a common tell, a body-language slip most people never realized they committed. Grant filed that away in the back of his head as he moved back into the kitchen and grabbed a bowl of potato chips. He returned to the lanai and set it in front of her, pleased by the flash of gratitude on her face as she dug her hand into the bowl.

"Here, I grabbed you a glass of ice water, too. It's hot out here."

"Thank you," she said, lifting the glass to take a sip. "Jeez, I feel like I ought to tip you or something."

"Simple applause will do," he said, returning to the grill. "So based on your career choice, I assume your aversion to marriage isn't because you don't believe in the institution.

What's your story?"

She shrugged and popped a chip into her mouth. "Like I said earlier, my parents divorced when I was young. The months leading up to it were really tough, with Mom and Dad fighting all the time. One night I heard them arguing and I went to the door of their bedroom and put a glass up to the door like I'd seen in a movie. You know, to eavesdrop?"

"Did you hear anything?"

He watched her fighting to keep her expression neutral, but she wasn't winning the battle. She took a sip of wine and looked out toward the ocean, her eyes distant. He studied her face, aware this was probably a story she didn't tell much, if ever. He edged closer, brushing the side of her shoulder with his hand.

"My dad said my mom hadn't been the same since they'd had kids—had *me*," she said. "And Janelle, of course." She swallowed, though she hadn't lifted the wineglass to her lips again. "And my mom yelled back that *he* was the one who'd changed. They started arguing about how their marriage had become nothing but a business arrangement devoted to car-pools and bake sales and soccer practice and whose fault it was they never spent time together. I didn't understand a lot of the conversation, but I got the gist."

"Jesus," Grant said, shaking his head. "You can't think—" He stopped short, knowing it would be a dick move to try and convince her that her parents hadn't split up because of her. Who the hell was he to rewrite someone else's story? He reached out and touched her arm. "I'm sure your parents loved you very much."

"I don't doubt that. But I also don't doubt that my very existence destroyed my parents' marriage."

"That doesn't mean it was your fault."

She shrugged and took another small sip of wine. "Realizing at age eight that you're responsible for the breakup of a marriage doesn't leave you feeling enthusiastic about the institution as a whole."

"So you just gave up on it?" His hand was still resting on her arm, and he wondered if she even noticed it there.

"No. For a while I still thought about it. Figured maybe a marriage without kids could be an option, or maybe just one where I worked really hard to make sure the romance wasn't dulled by the tedium of picking up someone else's socks. I fantasized about the fluffy white dress and the big bouquet of sunflowers and the Damascus steel band with one of those splotchy rustic diamonds on it."

"Wow. That's pretty specific."

She shrugged. "That's the nature of being a wedding planner. You learn what you love and what you don't. I suppose I became a wedding planner so I could start foisting all those fantasies on other people's weddings. Including my sister's."

He stood up and turned back to the grill, not wanting to miss a word of her story, but needing to flip the steaks. "Janelle's married?"

"*Was* married. To a guy who turned out to be a raging jerk. But I was too wrapped up in planning her big, fat, ridiculous wedding to notice."

"When was this?"

"The wedding was three years ago. The divorce is pretty recent. Still a lot of baggage there. The whole thing has really taken a toll on her."

"You can't seriously blame yourself for that."

"Why not? I pushed her into it."

"You can't *make* someone get married."

Anna shrugged and trailed a finger around the rim of her glass. "I'm pretty persuasive when I want something."

"I can only imagine." Grant turned and pulled the foil-wrapped potatoes out of the coals. He checked the steaks, making sure they were cooked to perfection. Satisfied, he returned to the kitchen and grabbed a bowl of baby carrots and some dip he'd bought at the store earlier. He nudged the fridge door shut and walked back to the patio, setting both items in front of Anna. She gave him a grateful smile and reached for a carrot.

"Aren't you being a little hard on yourself?" He turned and pulled the meat off the grill, sliding it onto a clean plate. "I'm guessing this wasn't an arranged marriage. Janelle had some responsibility for picking the guy, right?"

Anna shrugged. "It's a long story, and it looks like dinner's just about ready. Can we eat out here?"

Grant studied her for a moment, wondering if he should apologize for pressing her. She'd volunteered everything willingly enough, but maybe he'd been too pushy. She didn't look rattled, and she smiled at him as she stood up and smoothed out the front of her dress. Still, something had shifted between them.

"Sure," he said. "Eating outside is a great idea. Would you mind dusting off the table with that cloth there? I'll go grab everything."

He moved back into the kitchen and gathered silverware, napkins, coleslaw, and everything else he thought they might need. He considered grabbing the big citronella candle in the corner to help keep bugs away, but decided against it. No sense making her think he was trying to get romantic.

When he returned to the balcony, he saw she'd cleared off the table and laid out two bright orange plastic place mats his sister must've left behind when she last visited with the twins. They gave the table a festive look, and he set up the food feeling oddly jovial.

He sat down and began unwrapping his potato, glancing at Anna as she picked up her knife and fork.

"So," she said, slicing into the meat with a clean, even stroke. "So what's your secret?"

"Well, I usually pan sear the meat first to give it a nice even crust on the outside."

"Not the steak." Her eyes fixed on his, unblinking. "What you just did there."

He cocked his head to the side, studying her with renewed interest. "What did I just do?"

"The conversational equivalent of stripping off my clothes and having me on my back in the first thirty minutes of a date." She took a bite of steak and chewed, eyes never leaving his. Grant felt his mouth fall open, but no words came out.

Anna finished her bite and kept talking, her voice bright and calm and surprisingly cheerful. "Not that I didn't enjoy it," she continued, "and not that I didn't willingly spread my legs—metaphorically speaking, of course. But level with me here, Grant Patton—what the fuck was that about?"

Chapter Four

Anna waited politely while Grant choked on his wine. She should probably help him, but given how goddamn perfect he was at everything else, she figured he knew how to perform the Heimlich on himself.

"Are you always this blunt?" he asked when he finally got some air.

"Pretty much." She took a bite of steak and chewed. "Seriously, how did you do it? How'd you have me confessing my life story in less time than it normally takes me to remove my jacket?"

"You weren't wearing a jacket."

"You no doubt would have removed it if I were," she said. "Metaphorically speaking. Come on, Marine man. What the hell did you just pull to get me to tell you everything but the color of my underwear?"

The corner of his mouth quirked. "Fill in that last detail and I'll confess."

"Blue. To match the dress."

"And the streak in your hair." He took a long drink of water, then set the glass down and met her eyes. "Fair enough. What do you want to know?"

"What was that all about? Why did I just tell you my whole life story before I even knew your full name?"

"Grant Ulysses Patton. Our parents named us all after military generals. MacArthur, Grant, Sheridan, Schwartz— short for Schwarzkopf, as in Stormin' Norman."

"Your family isn't messing around with this military stuff."

"No doubt. Which might have something to do with my use of elicitation techniques in inappropriate settings like dates and job interviews. I apologize."

She blinked at him. "You used military-counterintelligence skills to get into my pants?"

"Are we still speaking metaphorically?"

"Yes. Why did you interrogate me?"

"It would only be an interrogation if I'd detained you, and I'd be using coercion tactics instead of evoking trust and comfort. Technically, this was more elicitation—a skill by which you acquire information without the subject realizing you're doing it."

Anna tried not to grin. "The *subject*? And here I've been dating guys who called me *honey* and *baby*."

"I didn't call you pet names, but I did ply you with a steady flow of refreshments. I also touched your arm and expressed sympathy for your misfortunes. That was genuine, by the way."

She shook her head and took another bite of steak. "That is seriously the most fucked-up form of foreplay I've ever heard of."

He studied her like he was trying to figure out if she was angry, amused, or crazy. It was certainly more of the last two, but she might as well keep him wondering. She picked up her butter knife and sliced into her potato. She felt his gaze on her as she loaded it up with sour cream and butter, along with a sprinkle of the fresh chives he'd grabbed from the potted plant beside the railing. Fresh chives? Christ, who was this guy?

"Even before the Marines trained me in counterintelligence, I had a knack for getting people to open up," he said. "It's always been like that. Even when I was a kid, random people just wanted to tell me things, confess secrets they didn't tell other people."

"I see," she said, taking a bite of potato. "So your career choices were either spy catcher or priest, and you were too big to fit in the confessional booth?"

He gave her a smile that looked almost guilty. "Pretty much."

"You're good, I'll give you that." She took another bite of potato, surprised by how fast she was devouring her dinner. Good Lord, this man was an amazing cook. An amazing *everything*, really. It was infuriating. And perplexing. And maybe a bit suspicious.

But it was mostly just sexy.

"So teach me something."

"What?"

"A technique. A way of making a bad guy reveal something he doesn't want to tell you. That's what you said counterintelligence means, right?"

"More or less." He considered her for a moment, then

nodded. "Okay, fine. Tell me a story that's a lie."

"What?"

"A story, but I want it to be a lie. Like maybe give me a detailed account what you did today, but lie about it."

"Okay." She thought about it. "Well, I started off my morning by getting a pedicure from Hugh Jackman. Then I went out and bought a new Mercedes and drove to Hana-lei Bay where I made love in the surf with George Clooney before meeting up with Daniel Craig for lunch. After that I went for a ride on the back of Bradley Cooper's Harley to teach a hula class to a bunch of school children, and then I watched the sunset from my private hot tub with Brad Pitt."

"You have a very good imagination."

"That's why I'm a weird wedding planner and not a priest or a spy catcher."

He took a sip of wine, his eyes never leaving hers. "So what did you do before lunch with Daniel?"

"What?"

"Your lunch with Daniel Craig. What did you do right before that?"

She frowned, trying to remember. "I think I was with Bradley Cooper. No, wait—"

"Or how about you tell me your whole day backward? What did you do last, and what did you do right before that, and what did you do before *that*?"

She grinned. "Okay, tricky guy. I can't do it easily, I'll admit. That's a technique?"

"Yep. Someone who's rehearsed a lie, or someone who's making one up on the fly only knows the story one way. But if you try to get him to tell it to you backward or from the middle or from someone else's point of view, a liar will stumble."

"What if the person just has a bad memory?"

"It's possible, which is why you're also watching for visual cues. There's a difference between someone who's concentrating on remembering the truth versus someone who's making up fiction."

"How do you mean?"

"You read someone's neurolinguistic indicators. For instance, you looked up and to the left when you were speaking. That can be a sign someone is accessing a part of the brain that fabricates fictional responses."

"Huh." She smiled, enjoying the game now that she knew what it was. "Do me again."

She watched his throat move as he swallowed. "Metaphorically speaking?"

"Right," she said, feeling a hint of heat creeping into her cheeks. "Come on, I want to learn some more of your secret spy-catcher skills."

He laughed and carved into his steak. "Okay, tell me another story that's not true."

"About what?"

"Anything. Just make something up. A total fabrication."

"All right." She took a final bite of her meal, then dabbed her napkin over her lips and set it atop the empty plate. "When I first met you on the beach yesterday, I was physically repulsed by your presence. Like, completely horrified. You're flabby and out of shape with no muscle tone to speak of, and your eyes are a ridiculous color." She paused, flicking her gaze over his massive biceps and chiseled chest, before returning to his eyes. Her stomach did a funny little somersault, but Grant didn't blink. Had she gone too far?

His expression was passive, and he said nothing, but he was nodding slightly.

She kept talking to fill the silence. "And of course, now that I've spent a little more time around you, I know you're a complete and utter dolt. You have no real talents like cooking or woodworking or home renovation, and you don't seem to have any admirable connection to your family." She pressed her lips together, but Grant kept nodding, a faint smile on his face.

"You have all these shelves around your house that are packed with books, which is a total bore—I mean, who likes a man who reads? And I saw the diploma on your wall in the office—magna cum laude?—please, no one likes an intelligent man, especially not one with great big hands and killer abs and a smile that could melt titanium on an ice rink. And don't even get me started on your complete lack of career ambition or failure to serve your country or community or charity or—"

"Are you finished?"

He was watching her with amusement in his eyes, so Anna managed a weak smile, even though the room felt a little spinny. "Actually, no. I could probably keep going awhile."

"I don't doubt it."

He leaned closer in his chair, so near now that their knees touched under the table. She could feel his breath rustling her hair, and she smelled something spicy and woodsy on his skin. The sun glinted in his hair, which was clipped close in a military buzz cut. What would it feel like to rub her palm over it?

He leaned closer, making Anna's breath catch in her

throat. What was it with this man and personal space?

And why did she want him in hers so very, very badly?

"Okay then," Grant said. "You just spoke about two hundred words. Generally speaking, that's three to four times more words than you would have uttered if I'd sat here quietly with my hands in my lap."

She stared at his hands, distracted by the size of them and the thought of what they could do to her and almost missed the fact that he was still talking. "Instead of doing that, I nodded as you spoke—three times in quick succession. It's a visual cue that lets you know I'm listening, I'm engaged, and I want you to keep talking."

"Right."

He leaned closer, near enough now that she could feel his shoulder brushing hers and the heat radiating from his chest, and she wanted to fall into that warmth. She forced herself to keep breathing.

"Another thing I did was not speak," he continued. "I didn't interrupt, I didn't ask questions, I just sat here. People don't like long silences—especially people who are uncomfortable with what they're saying—so they'll usually keep talking to fill the silence. Women in particular have an urgent need to fill silence."

His face was scant inches from hers now, and she watched his mouth in seeming slow motion as it formed the words "urgent need to fill." His pupils were wide and round, swimming in a sea of blue gray. He had faint stubble on his jawline, and she ached to know what it would feel like scraping against the hollow of her throat, the hollow between her legs—

"The other thing I did," he murmured. "Is invade your

personal space. It's one of the most disarming techniques."

She swallowed, her mouth suddenly dry. "You don't say."

"Is it working?"

"Uh-huh."

"Good. It's usually pretty effective."

"Oh?" Her voice was high and breathy and sounded distant to her own ears. Her blood was pounding hard in her head, in her fingertips, between her legs. Grant's eyes held hers, the tips of his fingers grazing the fine hairs on her forearms so lightly it might have been an accident.

She lunged for him, not sure if this was part of his plan, and not really caring. She had to have his mouth on hers, his hands on her body, his legs tangled with hers under the table or under a set of cool, sweaty sheets.

God, she wanted him.

He kissed her back, his lips softer than she imagined they'd be. He was slow at first, gentle, a man who knew how to take his time. It only made her hungrier. She urged him on, pressing her body against his as she cursed the damn chair arm that kept her from climbing into his lap and grinding against him like some kind of sex-starved animal.

His mouth moved down, and Anna closed her eyes to savor the scrape of his stubble rough against her cheeks, her lips, her throat, her shoulders. He seemed to be kissing her everywhere at once, his mouth and tongue hot and wet and so goddam perfect.

Of course he's a perfect kisser, too, her brain pointed out, sounding slightly snarky about it.

Not that the rest of her was complaining. One of his hands had drifted to her left thigh, fingertips toying with the hem of her sundress. He stroked her there, in no particular hurry, the lightness of his caress making her ache for more. Anna groaned as his touch grew firmer, his palm closing over her knee, engulfing it. His fingers stroked the tendon at the bend in her leg, taking their time, making her crazy. She kissed him harder, urging him on.

He moved the heel of his hand up just a fraction of an inch, sliding the hem of her dress out of his way. Anna raked her nails over the back of his skull, begging him without words to keep going. She let her knees fall apart, wondered if that was too forward, then decided she didn't care. She wanted him to touch her everywhere.

As if reading her thoughts, Grant let his other hand drift to her bare shoulder. His fingers tangled with the spaghetti strap on her sundress, slipping it down to reveal the curve of newly bared skin. He covered the flesh with his mouth, laying a trail of kisses along her collarbone. Anna cursed the tiny row of buttons up the front of her dress, wishing like hell they were snaps or Velcro or fucking nonexistent. She needed him to undo the goddamn buttons and bury his face between her breasts, sliding his tongue from one nipple to the other and devouring her like a starving man.

She also needed him to keep moving his hand up her thigh.

He's so goddamn perfect, why doesn't he have three hands?

Moaning a little in the back of her throat, she wriggled her fingers through the armrest and into his lap. Her palm grazed something hard and solid through the fabric of his shorts, and she used the points of her knuckles to stroke the length of him.

Good Lord. That's not a third hand, but it's certainly

bigger than a baby's arm.

She fumbled with his zipper, wanting to wrap her hand around him, to feel his length gripped snug in her palm. He moaned a little in the back of his throat. She felt him start to release her leg, and she drew her hand back and clamped it around his. Holding it in place, she drew back and met his eyes.

"Let me," she said, and reached for the front of her dress.

She fumbled with the first two buttons, then found her rhythm and undid three more, baring the tops of her breasts. Grant wasted no time moving his mouth to the naked expanse of skin, his free hand sliding the other shoulder strap down. Anna closed her eyes and breathed in the ocean air, heady with the caress of the evening breeze on her bare breasts. She'd never been so grateful for her less than ample chest, which meant going braless was totally an option.

Thank God for fewer layers, fewer hooks and buttons, and anything separating her from this man with the magical mouth.

Grant stroked her nipple with his left thumb, while his tongue made languid strokes over the other breast. She groaned and slid her hands into his hair—what little there was, she thought as she savored the soft prickle of his buzz cut under her palms. God, this man was a playground for her fingers. His scalp felt warm in her hands, and the things he was doing with his mouth—

"Oh, God, don't stop."

"Wouldn't dream of it," he murmured, his voice making pleasant vibrations against her sternum as his lips trailed from one breast to the other.

She let one hand stray down his back and nearly groaned

at the feel of all that muscle. Did this guy spend every waking hour at the gym, or was he just really gifted?

Really gifted, her brain telegraphed as his hand slid farther up her thigh, his thumb stroking her through her panties. She gasped, knowing how wet she was, how badly she wanted him, how urgently she needed his—

Ding-dong!

Anna opened her eyes and blinked, trying to orient herself amid the buzzing in her brain and the hum of pleasure pulsing through her body.

The chime sounded again, and Grant pulled his mouth from her nipple long enough to murmur, "Doorbell," against the underside of her breast.

Then he went back to kissing her, his mouth on hers again, the heel of his right hand brushing over her nipples. His left hand was buried under her dress, fingers sliding beneath the elastic of her panties. The tips of two fingers dipped inside her, sinking into her wetness as he stroked her with his—

Ding-dong!

"Oh, God," she gasped as the pad of his thumb found her clit, circling and sliding and making her crazy with heat. He buried two fingers deeper into her, using her wetness to glide and tease and stroke her to the brink of delirium. Anna closed her eyes again as his thumb circled faster, finding a rhythm as his fingers pulsed inside her and drew back, then pressed into her again. She gripped the back of his head, urging him on as he drew one nipple into his mouth, swirling his tongue around it in dizzying circles as Anna gasped and writhed and urged him to plunge deeper with his—

Ding-dong!

"Oh, for crying out loud!"

She opened her eyes and looked back through the house, thinking seriously about throttling whichever salesman or religious fanatic hovered out there on the damn porch. Grant sat up, blinking a little like a man coming out of a trance. He took a breath.

"I'm sure whoever it is will give up and go away," he whispered. "If it's important, they'd call."

"Right." Anna licked her lips. "Maybe we could sneak to the bedroom and—"

"Grant?" From the front of the house came a voice. A woman's voice. It was shrill and choked with something that sounded like tears, and Anna felt her blood run cold.

"Grant, are you home?" the woman cried again. "Oh, please—there's an emergency! I need you."

Chapter Five

Grant closed his eyes and counted to ten.

Okay, it was more like two. The panicked voice of the little old lady who lived next door was enough to send him sprinting into the house before the chime of the doorbell stopped echoing.

He grabbed the doorknob and hesitated, turning back to see Anna right behind him, buttoning up her dress. She was flushed and tousled and so goddamn beautiful he wanted to burn the house down to make the damn doorbell stop ringing.

Instead, he turned the doorknob.

"Oh, Grant—thank goodness it's you!" On the front steps, his plump, elderly neighbor stood blinking in the dusty sunlight on his porch. She wore an oversize pink chambray shirt that billowed around her like a big pink tent, and her chubby cheeks were flushed with terror. "Oh, dear, I just knew you were home, I heard voices a minute ago. I'm terribly sorry, dear, but—"

"Mrs. Stein," Grant said, throwing the door open all the way and pasting on his best Boy Scout smile. "What seems to be the problem?"

His gut tightened at the sight of the old woman's tear-streaked face. He scanned her from head to toe, looking for injuries before he turned his gaze to the street for potential assailants. He wasn't sure whether to reach for a pistol or a tissue. Behind him, he could feel the heat of Anna's body, and part of him still ached to grab her again.

Mrs. Stein began sobbing in earnest, which was enough to send all the blood rushing back to Grant's brain where it belonged. "Mrs. Stein," he tried again. "What is it, what's wrong?"

"It's Rumpymuffle. He's gone up a tree, and I don't know what to do. Oh dear, he's never been outside before, and the sun is going down soon. Help me!"

The woman wailed again and launched herself at the front of Grant's shirt. Given her considerable bulk, he had to brace himself to keep from toppling backward. He patted her shoulders, feeling faintly guilty about where his fingers had been just seconds before. He glanced at Anna, who had regained her composure and was looking on with an expression of intense concern.

Rumpymuffle? she mouthed.

"Her cat," Grant supplied. "Mrs. Stein, this is Anna Keebler. She's my sister's wedding planner. Anna, Mrs. Stein lives next door with a great big Maine coon who's never set foot outdoors."

Mrs. Stein drew back and sniffled. "I went to take the trash out and must have left the door ajar. I wasn't gone more than a minute, but something must have scared him and—well, look."

The old woman pointed to the large coconut palm that separated Grant's house from hers. Grant followed the direction of her finger, his gaze landing on the quivering form of Rumpymuffle gripping the tree for dear life.

"Shit," he muttered, then felt bad about it. "I mean *shoot*. He's at least twenty feet up there."

"I saw you had a ladder when you were painting your house, so I thought maybe—"

"No, that won't work," Grant said, eyeing the tree. "My tallest one is an extension ladder, but I can't brace that against a trunk that narrow. A rental shop might have an A-frame ladder that could work, but they're all closed at this hour."

The old woman began sobbing again, and Grant patted her back, thinking hard. He had a buddy with a small crane, but that was over on Oahu. Here on Kauai, he didn't know anyone with the sort of gear he'd need to get up that high, much less get down with a frightened cat. He looked at Anna again. Her eyes were big and round, and she was looking at him as though she expected him to be some sort of savior.

Far from it, babe.

His gut clenched. Part of him wanted to run. The rest of him was already forming a plan.

"Look, here's what we're going to do," he said, keeping his voice as soothing and upbeat as he could. "I'm going to run inside and see what I've got for gear. I did some jungle combat training at Camp Gonsalves in Japan. We learned to climb palm trees there."

Anna eyed him dubiously. "With an angry cat in your

hands?"

"With an M4 carbine with a collapsible stock. Probably not much different."

"Good point."

"Anna, can you hang out here with Mrs. Stein? Keep an eye on Rumpymuffle, and yell if he starts moving. I'll be right back."

He bolted into the house, his brain working on warp speed. He wished like hell he had some climbing gear, but he hadn't had much use for that on Kauai. *Gloves*, he thought, sprinting for the garage where he found a pair of bright gold work gloves with rubber grips on the palms and fingers. He started to grab for his work boots, then changed his mind. His feet were toughened from running on the beach, and he'd have a better grip without shoes.

He spotted a sturdy carabiner in his toolbox and grabbed that, his brain working through the logistics of climbing down with a squirrely cat in his arms.

Helmet, he thought, and frowned at his bike helmet. Not enough protection from falling coconuts, and there'd been several big ones in the tree. He sprinted back into the house and down the hall to the office where he found his grandfather's old McCord MI helmet from World War II. He grabbed it by the webbing and fastened it on, grateful Gramps had taken damn good care of his equipment. It might be an antique, but it still felt sturdy. He fastened it snug with the chin strap and knocked twice on the top to make sure it was solid.

He moved down the hall toward the bedroom, trying not to let his brain take a detour when he remembered Anna bent over the bed inspecting the carved headboard. Her ass

had been pert and perfectly round, the short dress riding up
to expose the tops of her thighs.

Don't think about that now.

Instead, he grabbed a laundry bag printed with bright
yellow ducks. His sister had given it to him as a housewarm-
ing gift, and it had a sturdy drawstring at the top. He turned
and yanked the top sheet off his bed and sprinted back outside. Mrs. Stein was at the base of the tree talking sweetly to
Rumpymuffle, who showed no sign of moving up or down.
His tail twitched a little, which seemed like a good thing
though what the hell did Grant know about cats?

A few feet away, Anna stood with her cell phone to her
ear. "Hang on, Mrs. Stein. I'm calling my friend, Kelli. She's
a veterinarian. Maybe she'll have some suggestions."

Good thinking, Grant thought, wondering why it hadn't
occurred to him to call Mac's new wife first thing.

*Because you want to be the damn hero. You need to save
the day.*

He shook off his inner voice as Anna turned to face
him. "No answer," she said, looking glum. "I forgot she and
Mac were going to the movies tonight. She's probably got
her phone off." She bit her lip and looked back up the tree.
"Mrs. Stein says Rumpymuffle takes special medication for
a thyroid condition. He's already a couple hours past when
he's supposed to take it. She's worried he'll get weak and
won't be able to hang on much longer."

"We'll get him down," Grant said. He held out the bed-
sheet. "Here, take this."

She raised an eyebrow at him. "This wasn't what I had
in mind when I imagined myself getting familiar with your
bedsheets."

"Later for that. You and Mrs. Stein can hold the corners and use it as a sort of rescue net."

"For you or for Rumpymuffle?"

"For the cat." Grant gave her a feeble grin. "If I fall, I'm pretty much on my own."

She bit her lip. "Are you sure this is a good idea?"

"No, but do you have a better one? The sun will be going down in a matter of minutes."

And I won't be, Grant thought, trying not imagine himself with his face buried between Anna's thighs.

She frowned, then shook her head. "I already tried the fire department. Apparently they're busy dealing with an actual fire."

"Okay then," Grant said, looking up the three. "Commence operation cat rescue in three, two, one — "

"Nice helmet," she said. "It goes great with your shoes."

"Thanks," he said, moving barefoot across the grass toward the massive palm. He pulled the carabineer out of his pocket and knotted the cinch string from the duck-printed laundry bag around it. Pulling it tight, he hooked the carabineer through his belt and clipped it shut.

"Wait," Mrs. Stein said, wriggling out of her pink chambray work shirt. You'll scratch your arms if you don't have long sleeves. Try this."

"I don't think — "

"Please," she insisted, thrusting the shirt at him. "It's the least I can do. Please hurry."

Seeing no point in arguing, Grant shrugged into the shirt. There was no way it would button around him, but he didn't need it to. He just needed protection for his arms. The oversized fit of it, coupled with the fact that Mrs. Stein probably outweighed him by forty pounds, meant the garment actually fit his shoulders pretty well.

"That's definitely your color," Anna said, managing a weak smile. "Between the gold gloves, the bare feet, and the helmet that looks like you stole it from a museum, you've got a head start on your next Halloween costume."

Grant offered her a mock salute and turned back to the tree. "I'll let you know when I'm ready to pose for the next issue of *Cat Rescuer* magazine."

He stood at the bottom of the tree and stared up, trying to remember what he'd learned in jungle training. No one was shooting at him, which was a plus, but doing this without any sort of climbing gear was probably not much safer.

"Are you sure about this?" Anna asked.

He turned to look at her, surprised by the look of concern in her eyes. Mrs. Stein sniffled and wiped a tear from her cheek.

"Yep," Grant said, and pulled on his gloves.

He turned back to the tree, eyeing the tree scars ringing the thick trunk. He reached around the tree and placed one palm behind it. He moved the other hand around the front of the tree at chest level, hugging the tree as tightly as its girth allowed.

He flexed his legs on either side and coiled himself to jump. He leaped up, the soles of his feet landing on either side of the trunk. He anchored his feet against the bark, his palms pressing tight from opposite directions, his feet doing the same from below.

Coiling his muscles, he sprang up with his legs, using them to push himself up the trunk frog-style. He squeezed the tree between his feet, extending his upper body up to find the next handhold. The tree bark bit into his palms, and he was grateful for the gloves as he clenched the tree between them. Hell, he was grateful for the stupid pink shirt, come to think of it.

Keeping his upper body affixed to the trunk, he used his legs to frog-hop upward again. He glanced beneath him, expecting to see more distance between himself and the ground. Six feet below, Anna gave him a timid little wave. Hell, she could probably jump up and grab his foot if she wanted to.

Don't think about Anna grabbing any part of your body right now, he commanded himself. *Focus.*

Grant turned his attention back to the tree trunk and leaped again, moving his hands upward. His legs followed, feet crawling slowly up the tree. The bark was biting into his knees, but he had a good grip. He hugged the tree tighter and moved up two more feet.

Don't lose your grip. They're depending on you.

He leaped again, finding his rhythm now. It had been years since jungle training, but the movement was feeling familiar. Not easy, and his wrists would be scratched to hell where the shirt was too short, but this was doable.

He was ten feet up the trunk now, and Rumpymuffle's fuzzy butt was in plain view above him. "Hang on, big guy," Grant called, trying to sound calm. "I'm coming for you, buddy."

Mew.

The kittenish sound gave Grant a sharp pang in his chest, and he hopped again, gaining another couple feet. He kept going, closer now, nearing the top where the branches split into leafy green fronds.

He could almost touch the cat.

Mew.

Rumpymuffle glanced over his furry shoulder, took one look at Grant, and skittered farther up the tree.

"Dammit," Grant muttered.

"Are you okay?" Anna yelled from below.

"Never better," he called.

"Please be careful."

The concern in her voice gave Grant the energy he needed for another surge up the trunk. He leaped again, just a foot from the frilled top of the palm. He let go with one hand and finessed his arm up through the palm fronds. Tugging a lower branch, he realized it couldn't possibly hold his weight. He stretched his arm higher, sweat pooling on his brow and dripping down his arms. His feet were killing him, and a boulder-sized coconut swayed dangerously over his head. His fingers found another branch and gripped it hard. Tensing every muscle in his body, he pulled himself upward through the branches.

Mew, said Rumpymuffle, glancing at him again.

"That's it, big guy. I've almost got you."

Grants legs were shaking with exertion now. His left foot slipped—probably from all the damn sweat—and he heard Anna gasp below him.

"Everything's fine," he called, regaining his grip and pushing himself higher. "Almost there."

Mew, the cat said again.

"That's right," Grant coaxed, letting go of the branch with one hand. He reached behind him and yanked on the mouth of the laundry bag, making sure he had a nice, wide opening. He grabbed hold of the branch, steadying himself, regaining his strength.

"Oh, dear," Mrs. Stein called. "Do be careful. You're so high up there."

Grant wasn't sure if she was talking to him or the cat, but it didn't matter. A fall from this height would be pretty fucking painful for either one of them.

Don't fall, he commanded himself.

He let go of the branch and stretched up, his fingers brushing the cat's soft fur.

"Shit, I need a few more inches."

He could've sworn he heard Anna mutter something beneath him, words that sounded a lot like, "Not from what I could tell," but he was probably imagining things. The damn heat was making him dizzy. He flashed on the memory of Anna's hand stroking him through his shorts, her knuckles grazing the head of his cock as she pressed his face into those beautiful breasts.

Dammit.

A hard-on was the last thing he needed right now. He took a steadying breath and reached for another branch. He tugged hard, making sure it could support his weight.

Thunk!

A falling coconut smacked hard on the top of his helmet, bouncing off and tumbling toward the ground.

"Watch out!" he called.

"Caught it!" Anna yelled. "Come down in one piece and I promise to make you my famous coconut-lime pie."

"Deal." Grant shook off the ringing in his ears and stretched upward again.

Still gripping the trunk between his feet, he pushed himself up once more. He caught another branch in his left hand

and yanked. The branch held, and no coconuts came raining down. He pulled himself up and let go with one hand.

"Let's try this again," he murmured to the cat. "On three. Ready? One, two—"

He stretched his fingers up and gripped the cat's scruff between his fingers and palm. "Three!"

He pulled back, peeling Rumpymuffle's claws off the trunk with an audible *scritch*. The cat yowled in protest, but didn't struggle. Thank God for small miracles.

"Here we go," Grant cooed, shoving the cat behind him into the bag. He couldn't see what he was doing, but he felt one set of claws snag in the fabric. He glanced over his shoulder, relieved to see Rumpymuffle's head had cleared the top of the bag. He let go of the cat and yanked the drawstring, cinching the bag shut.

Mrwow!

Twenty feet below, Anna and Mrs. Stein stretched the sheet out between them, holding it open like a net.

A net he probably hadn't washed for a couple weeks. God, if he made it down alive, he needed to seriously reevaluate how often he washed his sheets.

Don't think about that now.

Behind him in the bag, Rumpymuffle squirmed and hissed and sank a set of claws through the fabric. They connected with the back of his thigh, and Grant gave a yelp of pain.

"Dammit, cat. I'm trying to help you here!"

Slowly, cautiously, trying not to think about rabies shots, he began his descent down the tree. He slid both hands around the backside of the tree, hugging it tight as he released the pressure on his lower legs. He slid downward, letting his hands move with him. The cat was wriggling in the bag, making it tougher to balance.

He kept going, dropping faster than he probably ought to, but too damn eager to be back on solid ground.

Mrwow! the cat screamed again, sinking its fangs through the bag and into his right butt cheek.

"Shit!" Grant snapped, fighting the urge to unclip the carabineer from his belt and just let the cantankerous creature drop. "I mean *shoot*."

"You're almost to the ground," Anna cheered, her voice closer now than it had seemed minutes before. "Great work."

Grant inched his hands down again, leaning back a little as he slid his feet down the trunk again. The instant his feet touched the grass, Mrs. Stein was on him.

"Oh, baby! Oh, sweetie, Oh, honey, my precious little muffin."

Grant let go of the trunk and unclipped the bag from his belt, hoping like hell she was talking to the cat and not him. Mrs. Stein grabbed the bag and hugged it to her chest, tears streaming down her face as she began to loosen the knot at the top.

"You might want to wait till you're safely inside to let the cat out of the bag," Anna said. "I don't think Grant's going back up that tree if Rumpymuffle gets loose again."

"How can I ever repay you?" Mrs. Stein sobbed. "You saved my baby."

Grant smiled in spite of himself and tried to subtly rub the bite mark on his butt cheek. "Just doing my part to help out," he said. "I'm glad he's okay."

"Just let me get my checkbook. I owe you—"

"You don't owe me anything," Grant insisted, his voice a

little harsher than he meant it to be. "Just get that cat inside and give him a can of tuna. And a rabies shot."

"If you like, I can have my friend Kelli come take a look at him when she's free," Anna offered. "She makes house calls for friends."

"What would I do without the two of you?" Mrs. Stein sniffed again, while Rumpymuffle yowled from inside the bag. "Thank you. I mean it."

She turned and waddled back to her house, leaving Grant standing there in her pink shirt with a throbbing bite mark on his rear. When he turned back to Anna, she was studying him with an expression he couldn't read. It was either admiration or dismay, or some bizarre mix of the two.

She shook her head. "Unbelievable."

"What?"

"You're amazing. A true fucking Boy Scout."

He grinned and peeled off the pink shirt. He'd wash it later, fold it neatly, and return it to his neighbor. For now though, he had other things on his mind. He leaned close to Anna, his lips brushing her ear.

"In that case," he murmured. "Don't you think I deserve a merit badge?"

The flash of heat in her eyes made Grant forget all about the scratches on his wrists, the pain in his feet, the throbbing bite mark on his ass.

"You want a merit badge, huh?"

"Or something else."

She smiled. "The fact that your fly is already undone should facilitate the *something else*."

He looked down, appalled to realize she wasn't kidding. "What the hell?"

"Sorry, my fault." She grinned, not looking all that sorry. "I'm the one who unzipped it. I noticed when you started up the tree, but I didn't want to distract you."

Grant fumbled with the zipper, then stopped. "I don't suppose leaving it undone would be effective foreplay?"

Anna laughed. "I do want to get your pants off, but maybe not for that reason. Cat bites are vicious. You seriously need to have that looked at. Are you current on all your shots?"

"I can't vouch for Rumpymuffle, but the Marines keep me pretty up-to-date on my physical," he said. "Of course, it might not hurt to have you check it out."

She grinned and took a step back. "Tempting though that is, don't you think this is a bad idea?"

"Not particularly."

"The photography thing," she said, licking her lips. "If we might be working together, hooking up could make things awkward."

"Photography," he repeated, a little thrown to realize he'd completely forgotten the reason he'd invited her over.

Well, one of the reasons.

"I haven't even gotten to see your photos yet, but I'm sure they're amazing," she said. "Pretty much everything you do is flawless."

There was a slight edge to her voice now, a sound he hadn't heard before when she was purring in his ear. Grant studied her, trying to understand the sudden change.

"Why do you say that like it's a bad thing?"

"Sorry, I didn't mean it like that." She shook her head. "God, I sound like such a bitch. I guess I'm just a little discombobulated by you."

"Is discombobulated the same as turned on?"

She laughed, but the laughter didn't quite reach her eyes. "You're a little hard to believe, you know?"

Grant felt something sharp lodge in his throat. He tried to swallow it down, keeping his expression impassive. "What do you mean?"

"I just can't believe it—you cook, you read, you renovate homes, you do phenomenal woodwork, you serve your country, you donate to charity, you leap tall palm trees in a single bound to rescue a helpless animal and help an old lady. Is there anything you're *not* perfect at?"

Grant blinked, trying to decide if she was paying him a compliment or accusing him of something awful. Of what?

Trying too hard.

Being a complete and utter fraud.

Failing to make up for what you did.

He took a breath and folded his arms over his chest. No. She couldn't know any of that.

"I have a bite mark on my ass cheek and claw marks in my thigh," he said slowly. "If that's your idea of perfection, I hate to see what screwing up looks like."

She shook her head and smiled a little sadly. "Seriously, you're kind of unreal. Name one thing you're bad at. I'll bet you can't do it."

Grant froze, her words hitting him harder than she probably realized. He could think of a lot of things. So many failures, one in particular—

"I'm stubborn as hell," he blurted. "I have a terrible sense of fashion and home decor, so my sister helps me choose all my clothes and my dishes. I'm an obnoxious neat freak. I care too much what other people think of me—to a crippling degree, actually. I know absolutely nothing about wine, and can't distinguish between a two-dollar bottle of rotgut and an eight hundred dollar Pinot Noir. I am a hopeless procrastinator and overly ambitious, which can be a deadly combination at times."

He stopped, having run out of breath. She was staring at him with an expression he couldn't read, and Grant felt his heart stop.

At last, she smiled. "That's quite a list. I take it back. You really are a horrible person."

"You don't know the half of it."

His words hung there between them for a moment. She watched him, probably wondering if he was joking.

It's no joke. There's nothing funny about this at all.

Grant swallowed. "I suppose you're right."

"About what?"

"About the fact that we probably shouldn't sleep together. It would certainly complicate things. We've got my sister's wedding coming up, and if I might be working for you on several other weddings—"

"Right," Anna said, taking a step back. "That would be complicated."

"How about we just go back inside to look at the photos and call it a night?"

She glanced at the house, then back at him. "Here's the thing: if I go in there with you right now, I'll have my clothes off in five minutes."

All the blood drained from Grant's brain. "Remind me again why that would be bad?"

"And I'll be on my knees in front of you with my hand on your fly and—"

"You know, this blunt thing shouldn't be such a turn-on."

She smiled. "I'm just saying. If we've agreed to keep things professional, me going into that house with you right now would be a really dangerous thing."

"I'm a Marine. I'm used to danger."

She slugged him in the shoulder, not hard, but enough to leave him craving more of her touch. She sighed. "Seriously, how about you just email me some photos or something?"

"Tell you what," he said, trying to regain control of his libido. "You wait right here. I can dump a bunch of photos on a thumb drive for you. You have a laptop here in Hawaii?"

"Yes."

"Good," he said. "You can take the photos with you and look them over tonight. If you like what you see and you want me, I'm yours."

He heard the suggestive edge to his words the second they left his mouth, but he didn't take them back. Anna nodded, finding her voice at last. "That sounds good."

"Okay then," he said, stepping away from her and moving toward the house. "I'll grab your tote bag, too. You want to take home some leftovers for your sister?"

She shook her head. "You really are the perfect fucking host."

"Sorry. I'll work on being a bigger asshole."

She smiled. "Thank you."

Grant nodded and turned toward the house. He felt her gaze on his back and for an instant wondered if she could see right through him. See everything—the secrets, the lies, the betrayals.

He shook off her gaze and stepped through the door.

Chapter Six

Anna stood in the kitchenette of the little rental condo and began pulling things from her tote bag, her brain still reeling from her evening with Grant. Had she really walked away from the promise of hot sex with a perfect guy?

Is he really all that perfect, or is it an act?

Across the room, Janelle stood up and stretched as she made her way into the kitchen. "A coconut? A flash drive? A Tupperware container?" She studied the pile Anna had made on the counter. "Is that a handbag or a clown car?"

"The slaw is for you. The coconut is for pie. I'll give you a piece if you're nice."

Janelle grinned. "From the beard burn on your throat, I'd say Grant must've been very nice. Did you give *him* a piece?"

Anna swatted at her sister with a dish towel, but Janelle danced out of the way, laughing. "Oh, come on—dish!" Janelle urged. "I want to hear all about it."

"There's nothing to tell," Anna said, turning her back as she shoved the slaw into the fridge and tried to cool her flaming face. "Yeah, we might have fooled around a little, but we decided it was a bad idea."

"Why on earth would it be a bad idea to tongue-wrestle with a sex god?"

"Because we're trying to maintain a professional relationship."

And also because I've got the world's worst track record when it comes to judging men and relationships, Anna amended silently as she busied herself trying to find something she could use to crack the coconut.

"So he's going to be our wedding photographer?"

"I'm not sure yet. I need to look at his photos."

Janelle quirked an eyebrow at her. "You've been gone three hours. I thought you went over there to look at his portfolio. What the hell were you doing that whole time?"

"Touring his house, eating dinner, watching him scale a thirty-foot palm barefoot with his fly undone."

"Okay, now I'm intrigued. You didn't even mention the tongue-wrestling in there, so I know you're leaving stuff out. Come on, tell me everything."

So Anna did, omitting few of the more intimate details of their near-miss hookup, but covering nearly everything else. When she finished, her sister was gawking at her.

"Holy shit, I take back what I said about him being a sex god. I think he might actually *be* God. Did you happen to see any white robes or a big gold scepter?"

"I didn't look, but I'm not taking any chances. I think sex with the Almighty might actually kill me."

"Yeah, but what a fun way to go. Maybe after all the

weddings are over—"

"No." Anna's voice came out a little too sharp, and she tried to cover it with a smile, but Janelle hadn't missed it.

"Methinks the lady doth protest too much."

"That's the other thing—his bookshelves were lined with things like Shakespeare and Plato. How could you ever fart in front of a guy like that?"

Janelle frowned. "I think I missed something here."

"I'm just saying," Anna said, giving up on the coconut and palming the flash drive instead. "Being with a guy who's too perfect would be exhausting. I don't have it in me."

"Speaking of having it in you—"

"Cut it out, you little pervert. Let's look at the sex god's photos."

Janelle shrugged and padded over to the little table where they'd left the laptop charging. She flipped it open and held out her hand for the flash drive. Anna handed it over and dropped into the seat beside Janelle, not sure why she felt so fluttery inside. It was ridiculous. She was a grown woman who'd dated plenty of smart, creative, professional men with—

"Wow, that's a really long one!"

Anna blinked, her libido surging traitorously at her sister's words. "What?"

"Exposure. A long exposure. That's what he must've used to get this shot of the night sky." Janelle looked up from the monitor and grinned. "What did you think I meant?"

"Exposure, obviously." Anna cleared her throat and pulled the laptop closer to her so she could have a better view. "Wow, that really is a great shot."

"Isn't it?"

She scrolled through a folder of landscape photography, admiring Grant's skill at capturing sunsets and lakes and raindrops on blades of grass. She hadn't pegged him as the artistic type, but he sure as hell had a knack for composition.

"Let me drive," Anna said, seizing control of the computer and clicking to a subfolder labeled "bugs."

She expected photos of insects, maybe beautiful butterflies or lightning bugs at sunset.

"What the hell is that?" Janelle asked.

"Surveillance equipment of some sort. That's what you get when a Marine counterintelligence expert labels a folder 'bugs.'" Anna tapped on a close-up image of some sort of microchip stuck to the bottom of a saltshaker. It was surprisingly artistic, rendered in black and white with great contrast and detail.

"The guy could take a creative shot of a bowl of potato soup," Janelle said. "He's got an amazing eye."

Anna nodded and clicked on another photo, transfixed by a breathtaking image of a shirtless man in combat fatigues cradling an infant to his chest while a smiling woman peered over his shoulder. That one was in a subfolder labeled "friends," so the guy in the photo must be a fellow Marine holding his new baby. Anna clicked another picture, spellbound by the detail and character and personality Grant had managed to capture in each image. A woman in a raincoat on a misty street corner. A soldier offering water to a bedraggled dog. Dirty, dark-haired kids dancing in the spray from a fire hydrant.

"He's really good," Anna murmured, not sure why she was surprised. The bastard was great at everything.

"I want to see those pictures of your friend—Kelli? The

one who married Grant's brother. You said Grant took the engagement photos?"

"Right, I'm sure he threw them in here somewhere." She clicked a folder marked "family" and spotted a subfolder labeled "Mac and Kelli engagement."

"I'm going to go out on a limb here and guess this is it," she said, clicking it open. "Here, look at this one—notice the way he captured the light on her face."

"She looks so in love."

"Kinda what you want in a wedding photographer. Check this one out—it's one of the only times I've ever seen Mac without sunglasses."

"Wow," Janelle breathed. "Can you imagine what it would be like to have a guy look at you like that? Like you're the best, most amazing thing that's ever happened to him."

Something caught in Anna's throat, and she found herself blinking hard against the glare on the computer screen. At least she thought it was the glare.

"I can't imagine," she said softly and clicked the folder closed. "Let's see what else he's got."

"What do you think is in that one?" Janelle pointed to a folder marked "Desiderium."

Anna shrugged, hovering the mouse over the folder. "Is that a woman's name?"

"If it is, it's a weird one."

"The Patton family is funny with names. All the kids are named after military generals, but maybe he's got cousins who are all named with Latin words for body parts or something."

Anna began through the images in the folder. At first, they seemed not to match the rest of the shots on the zip drive. Many of them were grainy, looking like poorly scanned versions of old Polaroids. In one shot, two young boys with matching gray eyes stood shoulder to shoulder in red-and-white baseball uniforms. One held a bat and the other held a glove. Both were missing a front tooth, which wasn't the only thing about their smiles that matched.

"Grant's brothers?" Janelle guessed.

"Grant," Anna said, not sure why she was so certain. "He's the one on the left. The other one must be a brother, but I don't think it's Mac. Mac has brown eyes like Sheri and their mom."

She clicked the next one in the series and opened an image of the same two gray-eyed boys looking a little bit older.

"Oh, wow!" Janelle laughed. "Is that Grant's homecoming picture?"

"He must have double-dated with his brother," Anna said, studying the poofy-haired blonde girls flanking them like bookends. "Geez, even their dates match."

Anna kept clicking, watching as Grant's high school years unfolded before her eyes, always with his brother beside him. The images moved through their college years, then into a series of shots showing the young men in military attire.

"That's not Mac in any of those?" Janelle asked.

"No," Anna said, clicking open a photo that showed two young men in military garb. "Mac's hair is darker. Besides, that's an Army uniform. Mac was a Marine, just like Grant is."

"So who—"

"The other brother. One they don't ever seem to talk

about. Grant mentioned him over dinner."

"He's in the Army?"

"I have no idea. Grant didn't tell me much. Just that he's not in touch with the family a whole lot. I guess if he's the black sheep of the family, it would make sense he'd pick a different branch of the military than Mac and Grant did."

Anna clicked another photo, this one showing Grant and his brother shirtless on a beach, tossing a football between them. Both were glorious specimens of masculinity, tan and muscular with the close-cropped hair and the rippling muscles of young, professional soldiers.

Janelle eyed her curiously. "Since when are you an expert on military families?"

"I got to know Mac when I worked on his wedding to Kelli. As well as anyone knows Mac, anyway. Kelli calls him Tall, Dark, and Detached from Humankind."

She clicked another photo, this one of the two brothers in more formal military attire. Each had an arm slung around the other's shoulders, and they were laughing at something outside the reach of the camera's lens.

Anna clicked the last photo in the series and froze.

It was a shot of the mysterious brother alone. This photo was more artistic than the others, rendered in black and white with dark shadows everywhere. The brother was hunched on a battered chair, his body turned away from the camera. His hair was a disheveled mess, and one hand was clenched in a fist at his side. He had several days' worth of stubble on his jaw, and a frown that formed harsh brackets around his mouth.

The image looked candid, and he must have turned his head toward the photographer just as the shutter clicked.

There were lines in his face that hadn't been there in any of the other photos and a haunted look in his eye that made Anna shiver.

"Wow," Janelle said. "There's something really depressing about that one."

"No kidding."

"He's beautiful though," Janelle murmured, her voice a little trancelike. "*It's* beautiful, I mean. The photo. Well, so is the man. Where did you say he lives?"

"I didn't." Anna swallowed. "I don't know anything else about him."

"That's one dark and broody man."

Something in Janelle's voice made Anna tear her gaze off the photo and focus on her sister's face.

Janelle blinked. "What?"

"Nothing. You look a little—transfixed."

"I can't help it. There's something about this guy."

"Right." Anna swallowed and reached for the mouse.

Janelle cleared her throat. "So Mac is the stoic, badass brother and this guy in the picture is the tortured-looking black sheep. What does that make Grant?"

Anna clicked the photo shut and watched it vanish from the screen. She'd known Grant less than twenty-four hours, but she could list at least a dozen adjectives to describe him. Smart. Kindhearted. Helpful. Heroic. Charitable. Cheerful. Accomplished.

But something about that photo made her think there was another side to him.

"Full of secrets," she said, feeling uneasy. She pushed the laptop closed, wondering if she'd find out what lay behind Grant Patton's perfect, polished surface.

. . .

Anna was brushing her teeth before bed when her phone rang. She glanced at her watch, surprised to realize it was earlier than she expected. Apparently she hadn't adjusted to the three-hour time difference between Portland and Hawaii.

Her phone was half covered by a hand towel, and the sight of "Patton" on the readout made her heart do a pitiful little leap in her chest.

She shoved the towel aside, switching gears when she saw "Sheri" instead of "Grant."

"This is Anna," she said, cradling the phone between her shoulder and cheek.

"Hey, Anna, it's Sheri. Sorry to call so late, but I wanted to let you know Sam and I finally made a decision on the cake."

"You went with the white cake and buttercream frosting, filled with layers of strawberry?"

Sheri laughed. "You're a psychic wedding planner as well?"

"Nah, the bakery called and told me you two stopped by. Excellent choice, by the way. I'll make sure the bakery has everything set up that afternoon just like you want. I just checked the tracking info on your custom cake topper, and that should be here by tomorrow afternoon. I'll call the bakery tomorrow to make sure they have it."

"Thanks, Anna. God, this is so much easier having a wedding planner. I'm so glad Kelli recommended you."

"Not a problem. It's my job to make your life easier so

you can enjoy your big day."

"I'm determined to do that this time around. My first wedding was a disaster, with my mom and me staying up all night to make a million of these stupid little bows for the back of the guests' chairs while my ex snored in the other room. That probably should have told me something right there, huh?"

"I'm glad you're getting a second shot to do things the way you want," she said, not sure whether she was talking about the wedding or the marriage.

"It's so nice to leave the wedding details to someone else so I can focus on enjoying the groom."

There was a muffled giggle on the other end of the line, and a baritone voice mumbling something salacious about enjoying the groom. Sheri laughed again, and a ridiculous pang of jealousy nipped at the corner of Anna's brain. She pushed it aside, forcing a smile into her voice.

"I'm so happy for the two of you. Grant mentioned Sam asked him to be the best man, so I assume we're all squared away on the wedding party now?"

"Yep. Totally fitting, don't you think?"

"What do you mean?"

"Grant as the best man. Aside from my betrothed, he's the best man I know. He said he volunteered to photograph some weddings for you?"

"We're still discussing it, but I won't let him volunteer. Obviously, I'll insist on paying him."

"Good luck with that. The man is a consummate volunteer. If you ever need a kidney, put him on your short list of people to ask."

Anna considered the idea of asking Grant for a body

part and decided it wasn't his kidney she wanted. She cleared her throat.

"He's a very skilled photographer," Anna said. "Not much experience shooting weddings, but he clearly has an eye for capturing human interaction. I think he'll be great at it."

"I'm surprised he's so eager to do it. The man's spent his whole adult life running like hell at the sound of wedding bells, but maybe it's different when they're someone else's."

Anna twisted the hand towel around her fingers, focused on keeping her voice nonchalant. "Some people just don't have the urge to get married."

"I suppose, though Grant would be great at it. He's dated plenty of amazing women—lots of beautiful, fluffy blondes in sweater sets, which sounds a little boring when I put it that way. Total Stepford wives, but Grant's out of there at the first sign one of them wants to make the wife thing the real deal."

Anna stole a glance at the mirror and studied her reflection. She stood braless in a tank top that read "Wedding planning's not for pussies," a gift from a former client. The blue streaks in her red-gold hair shone wild and bright under the florescent bathroom lights, and the sunflower tattooed on her left shoulder blade seemed larger than normal.

Stepford wife she was not. She was mostly happy about that, but she knew the real reason for her need to squelch anything traditional in her attitudes and demeanor. She didn't deserve the traditional happily ever after, so she'd make damn sure she shied as far away from traditional as possible.

"Anyway," Sheri continued, cheerfully unaware of her wedding planner's critical self-analysis, "I'm glad he's going to be taking photos for you. He's always had such a talent for it, but this will stretch his comfort zone a little."

Anna thought about those photos on the flash drive. Something told her he hadn't meant to include them. That they were something private, even sacred. Was there a way to learn more from Sheri without giving away any of Grant's secrets?

You don't know any secrets, her subconscious argued. *He's made sure of that.*

Anna cleared her throat. "Have you ever heard of Desiderium?"

"Desiderium? I don't think so. Wait, is that the vibrator that plugs in? Kelli bought me one after my divorce."

"Right," Anna said, pushing aside the memory of the brother's haunted eyes in that last photograph and focusing on the discussion at hand. "Desiderium. It's the latest rage among all my brides this year."

. . .

Grant wasn't surprised when Anna called the next day and offered him the wedding photography job. He'd known his work was solid, and besides that, she was in a bind.

What surprised him was the aloofness in her voice.

"So I'll pick you up at noon?" she said, sounding businesslike instead of like a woman who'd spread her thighs and urged him to slide his hand up her dress.

"Noon," Grant repeated, still distracted by the memory of her thighs and the way she'd felt slippery around his fingers, the soft whimpers forming low in her throat and making him want to bend her over the table and slide hard and deep into her. "Um, yeah. That works for me."

After a few minutes of squabbling about money—Anna insisting she needed to pay him, Grant insisting he owed her some free work after maiming her original photographer—they hung up and Grant went to take a shower.

Anna arrived at noon on the dot. He looked at her through the peephole, admiring the curve of her small breasts beneath a pale sea-green sundress. She was biting her lip and holding a pie plate in her hands.

When Grant opened the door, she thrust the pie at him.

"What's this?" he asked, admiring the little flecks of coconut and lime zest on the custardy-looking surface.

"Coconut-lime pie," she said. "You're not the only passably skilled cook around here. I made it with the coconut that beaned you in the head. You should stick it in the fridge."

"My head or the pie?"

"Both." She laughed and tucked a strand of hair behind her ear, the blue streaks flashing in the sunlight. What the hell was it about her that was so damn intriguing?

"Your condo must have an oven?"

"No, it's a no-bake pie," she said. "I'll give you the recipe sometime."

"Thanks. That's really sweet of you."

God, they were exchanging recipes now? He'd been seriously friend-zoned if that was the case. It was best, he knew, but the thought made him glum.

Grant turned away and moved toward the kitchen to shove the pie in the fridge. He grabbed his camera bag and returned to the door.

"Ready to roll?"

"After you," he said, and let her lead the way to her rental car.

Grant thought about offering to drive. Hell, he knew this island better than she did, and the macho part of him liked being behind the wheel. But Anna seemed like the sort of woman who liked being in the driver's seat, too, which was fine by him. He needed a few minutes to get his camera gear organized.

"So this is the wedding with the fairy-tale theme?" Grant asked, settling into the passenger seat with his bag on his lap.

"Yes. Only the bride's family convinced her to go a little more traditional. Instead of gnome costumes and bridesmaids with wings, we're doing the ceremony at a private lodge near Hanalei Bay so they can play off the 'Puff the Magic Dragon' concept. You know, 'He frolicked in the autumn mist in a land called—'"

"Hanalei, got it," he said, feeling oddly charmed by her tuneless singing. And by the jangly bracelet around her ankle, the one without the tattoo. And by pretty much everything else about her, come to think of it.

"So nontraditional weddings are your bread and butter," he said, unscrewing the filter from his lens.

"Pretty much. I do normal weddings—your sister's, for instance—but most people seek me out because I'm known for being a bit unusual."

"You don't say."

She glanced at him then, her expression wary, like she was trying to figure out what he meant. "Hey, it wasn't an insult," he assured her. "I think it's cool you march to the beat of your own drum. You're not like a lot of women."

"How do you mean?"

He shrugged, knowing he should probably tread carefully here or risk insulting her. He wiped down the filter with a dust-free cloth as he considered his words. "The bluntness, for one. A lot of women play games or beat around the bush with what they mean to say, but not you. You just put it all out there, brutal honesty and all."

"Honesty," she repeated, giving a firm nod. "Yep."

"And your career is sort of your own unique thing. Same with your hair, your jewelry, the tattoos. You're definitely your own person."

She was smiling a little now, warming up to the idea that he wasn't insulting her. Grant wiped down the lens and kept going.

"You're funny. I love your sense of humor, and that cute dimple that shows only when you smile really big."

She rewarded him with a bigger grin, and Grant started to feel warm all over.

"Observant," she said. "Most people don't notice I only have one dimple."

"On the right. I noticed. It's very unique." He set the dust-free cloth aside and pulled out his handheld blower. "Then there's the marriage thing."

"Marriage thing?"

"So many women your age are dying to get hitched. To have the big froofy wedding and the traditional family with 2.3 kids and a house in the suburbs. But that's not what you're after."

There was the tiniest falter in her smile. So tiny he might have imagined it, or maybe she was frowning at the wild rooster squashed on the side of the road.

"Right," she said, flashing him a grin that made him certain he'd misread her a second ago. "Definitely not looking to walk down the aisle at any point in my life."

"I think that's cool," he said. "Same here."

"Oh?"

"I'm not a fan of marriage. It's fine for other people, but not for me."

"What happened to you?"

Grant blinked, a little surprised by the directness of the question. There had to be some point where he'd stop being caught off guard by her blunt nature, but he wasn't there yet.

"What do you mean?" He was trying to keep his tone light and casual, but knew he wasn't doing a very good job of it.

"People who don't want to get married usually have a reason for it," she said, glancing at him from the corner of her eye. "Their parents' divorce, screwing up their sister's marriage—things like that."

"Hypothetically speaking?"

"Right. So what's your story? Why don't you want to get married?"

"Are you proposing?"

He meant it as a joke, a way to keep the conversation lighthearted and whimsical and away from anything serious.

But from the way she cut her eyes to him, he knew he'd missed the mark. He swallowed and went back to dusting his camera lens.

"I don't have a story."

Anna went quiet. For a moment, he thought they'd reached the end of the conversation. He started to relax, went back to using a little handheld blower to puff air into the camera body. He was still looking down in his lap when he felt the car jerk to a stop.

He looked up to see Anna staring at him over the rim of

her sunglasses. "For a guy who says he admires honesty and bluntness, you sure have a helluva hard time being forth-coming with those qualities on your own."

"What?"

She shrugged. "I just think there's more to you than you're letting on. Something darker. Something that's not all cheerful Boy Scout."

Grant swallowed, not sure what to say to that. What was she driving at? Did she know something?

"Come on," Anna said, shoving her sunglasses back up her nose as she opened the car door. "The wedding party's waiting."

"We're here already?" He glanced around, surprised to realize they'd already reached Hanalei.

"Yep." She swung her legs out of the car and stood up, then peered back down at him. "Let's get the ball rolling on the blessed union of holy matrimony. Or as you and I can regard it, 'I'm glad it's them and not us.'"

"Us," Grant repeated under his breath, grateful she'd already walked away.

Chapter Seven

"I now pronounce you man and wife. You may kiss the bride."

Anna beamed the way she always did at the pivotal moment in the ceremony, her eyes prickling with happy tears. Beside her, Janelle began clapping along with the other guests. She leaned close to whisper in Anna's ear.

"That was awesome."

Anna nodded, pleased another wedding had gone off without a hitch. "It was, wasn't it?"

"I thought it might bother me to hear that so soon after the divorce, but that was beautiful."

"It never gets old," Anna said. "No matter how many times I hear it."

"I can see why. It's the epitome of hope, you know?"

"Hmm," she murmured, glancing around to make sure Grant was capturing the couple's lip-lock. She spotted him on the other side of the arch, kneeling a few feet from the bride and groom and framing the shot to make sure Hanalei

Bay was visible in the background. "Perfect."

"Oh, I don't know," Janelle said, following Anna's gaze to Grant. "I saw him scratch his balls in the middle of the ceremony."

"You did not!"

"No, but wouldn't you like him more if I had? The man needs a few chinks in his armor."

"Come on," Anna said, pulling her sister by the arm. "Let's make sure the baker knows how to set up the cupcake tree."

"And by that you mean 'let's sample a couple?'"

"It's a professional obligation. I need to make sure everything's just so for the bride and groom."

From the corner of the buffet station, Anna watched Grant work the crowd. He seemed to know instinctively to capture an image of the groom stooping to retrieve the bride's dropped fork, followed by a shot of the bride playfully smacking the groom's butt as he bent down. The couple's laughter rang out across the lush grounds, making Anna feel oddly wistful.

She watched Grant's biceps flex as he slung his camera bag over one massive shoulder and moved to the other side of the reception area. The sun glinted in his hair, and he had the self-aware stride of a guy confident in every step he took.

It would be infuriating if it weren't so goddamned sexy.

Anna had just polished off her third mini-cupcake when Grant found her an hour later beside the cupcake tree.

"Sampling the goodies?" he said, firing off a shot as Anna wiped frosting from her chin.

Anna grinned and swallowed a mouthful of pineapple cupcake. "They're going to have a ton left. The baker accidentally made five dozen extras, so we've got three more boxes of them in the catering van over there."

"I see. So you're devouring a few to help out the happy couple."

"It's a hardship, but someone's gotta do it." She grinned and dusted crumbs off her hands as she watched Grant take a bite. "Delicious, isn't it?"

"Oh my God, what is this?"

"Lilikoi—also known as passion fruit—with guava frosting. Isn't it tasty?"

"Amazing."

"I helped the bride pick them out last week, so I got to try all the flavors then. My favorite was orange ginger with a lavender-lemon frosting, but the bride didn't pick that flavor."

"That sounds delicious. I've never been to a wedding that had cupcakes instead of a regular cake."

"It's become very popular. Terrific idea, if you think about it. You can have a dozen different flavors if you like, and everyone gets to try everything."

Grant nodded and swallowed his bite of cupcake. "You're really good at what you do, aren't you?"

Anna blinked, surprised. "Yes. I am, as a matter of fact."

He grinned. "I love your honesty."

"Well, you asked the question. I've worked really hard to build a successful business."

"And you're passionate about marriage."

"About weddings," she corrected, ignoring the knot in the pit of her stomach. "There's a difference."

He nodded, eying her curiously. "That there is. So what happens now?"

For one stupid moment, she thought he meant *with us,* and the words settled warmly in the center of her chest. *Us.* But that was ridiculous. There was no *us,* for crying out loud.

She swallowed. "What happens next with the wedding, you mean?"

"Yeah. Is there more to shoot?"

"It's totally optional for you, but the wedding party and all the guests are heading off into the jungle for a rousing game of Fairies in the Forest."

"Fairies in the Forest?"

"Don't ask me. I think it's a little like hide-and-go-seek, but for weird people."

"In that case, lead the way." He grinned. "I didn't mean that the way it sounded."

"Yes you did, but that's okay. Come on, I think most of them went this way."

She grabbed his arm and felt an instant jolt of electricity move from her fingers to the place she'd stroked with her fingers while lying alone in bed last night. She'd been picturing Grant then, imagining him between her legs with her ankles locked behind his back and his perfect ass moving in rhythm as he pumped into her with—

"You want me to get shots of the guests, or just focus on the bride and groom?"

"Um—how about whoever you can find? I'm not really sure where everyone went, so just follow the sound of voices and start snapping." They'd reached the edge of the jungle now, and Anna could hear shrieks of laughter that sounded like the bride.

Grant turned to her and smiled. "You planning to hide?"

"Me?"

"Your job duties are mostly done now, right?"

"More or less. Janelle's managing the cleanup crew, and the caterer has everything handled for the reception."

"So go hide. You might as well enjoy the fun and games, too, right?"

Anna wasn't sure why she felt the urge to obey, but it probably had to do with the man issuing the command. Grant could ask her to cover her body in maple syrup and pretend to be a waffle, and she'd eagerly lie down on a plate for him. Or anywhere.

"Okay," she said. "Whatever you say. Except maybe the waffle thing."

"What?"

"Never mind. If you haven't found me in fifteen minutes, I'll assume you got caught up taking pictures."

"If I haven't gotten all the Fairy in the Forest pictures in fifteen minutes, you have permission to punch me in the crotch."

He turned and walked off before Anna could give too much thought to the idea of having her hand between his legs. He shot a grin over his shoulder at her as he headed deeper into the jungle.

Anna watched him go, then turned and made her way toward the ocean. The wedding site was high up on a cliff above Hanalei Bay, with the jungle fanning out behind it in a web of lush greenery and singing birds. The scent of plumeria drifted across the breeze, and Anna combed her fingers through her hair, enjoying the way the salty sea air added waves to the otherwise stick-straight strands.

She stepped around a fallen palm frond, making her way toward the cliff's edge. She glanced down at her cell phone, relieved to see no messages from the DJ or florist or anyone else having a wedding-related crisis. She felt her shoulders start to relax as distant laughter rang out through the trees.

The couple was happy. The wedding had gone off without a hitch, and if Anna's instincts were right, Grant had gotten some great shots. True, he was a lot different from the regular photographers she worked with. Once when he knelt down to get a shot, she realized he looked more like a man aiming an assault rifle than a Nikon, but none of the guests had said anything.

She smiled as she pictured him in her mind, his broad shoulders straining the fabric of his blue linen shirt, ripples of muscle showing beneath the material. God, what would it be like to rake her fingernails over that much flesh? Had she ever been with a man that big, that hopelessly fit? The thought was both intimidating and thrilling.

She stepped around some sort of leafy tropical plant as the view of the bay opened up below. She stopped short on the ledge and gasped.

"Oh," she murmured, scanning the view.

There wasn't a cloud in the sky, and the ocean sparkled like aquamarines glinting in a shower of sunbeams. A little sailboat bobbed on the horizon, and surfers rode white-capped waves to the sandy fringe of the beach.

A thick cluster of greenery trailed up from the shore on the opposite side, and Anna spotted a little white cottage nestled among the palms. Its windows glinted in the sunlight, taking in the sweeping ocean views, while the jungle behind it cradled the little house in privacy. The effect was breathtaking. Cozy. Romantic. A beautiful place for a wedding and a honeymoon.

You could have a small, private ceremony in the courtyard off to the side over there, with a bouquet of sunflowers and a mantilla veil and those orange-ginger cupcakes and Janelle beside you wearing—

She frowned, shaking herself out of the fantasy.

It'll never be you. You've already had too many chances. That sort of happily ever after isn't meant for someone with your judgment.

With a sigh, she sat down on the edge of a large, weathered log and looked out at the house. Then she pulled her eyes away and went back to watching the sailboat inching its way across the horizon.

She wasn't sure how long she'd been sitting there when she heard the rustle of footsteps behind her. She turned to see Grant striding toward her with a camera around his neck. He smiled when he saw her.

"Tag. You're it."

"Wrong game. I think you're supposed to say, 'Sunbeams and light, you're a silly sprite,' then spin in a circle five times for Fairies in the Forest."

"How about I take a rain check and just enjoy the view?" He eased himself down onto the log beside her and gave a low whistle. "Amazing, isn't it?"

"It is. The happy couple chose well." Anna scooted over a little on the log to make room for him. One of his massive shoulders brushed hers, and she fought the urge to sink her nails into it. "Did you get lots of pictures?"

"Yep, check it out."

He flipped the camera around so she had a good look at the viewfinder. She leaned closer, her knee grazing his as he shifted his body so his elbow brushed the side of her breast.

If he noticed, he didn't say anything. A perfect gentleman.

"I got a great shot of the flower girl trying to give the ring bearer a wedgie," he said, scrolling through the images. "And look at this one of the bride's parents kissing behind a palm tree."

"Wow," Anna breathed, reaching for the button to scroll backward through the day's shots. "These are terrific, Grant. Really. I'm impressed with your talent. Not surprised, but impressed."

"Thanks." He grinned at her. "It was fun."

"Yeah?"

"More fun than I thought it would be. Good practice for Sheri's wedding, even though I don't get to be behind the camera for that one."

"You'll be a great best man," Anna said, looking up from the camera to see his face darken. "It'll be nice to see you working a wedding in a different role."

"Right," Grant said, frowning. "I'm looking forward to it."

Like hell you are, Anna thought, but said nothing. She handed the camera back to him and smiled. "Nice work."

"Thank you." He stuffed the camera back in his camera bag and zipped it up.

"I looked at all the pictures on the flash drive you gave me," she said, wondering if she should ask about the brother in the photo. "There was a lot of variety."

"I dumped most of my photo files on there. Probably should have taken a little time to organize things better."

"No, it was great. There was some family stuff on there."

Grant nodded, shifting a little on the log beside her. "Mac and Kelli's engagement photos, right. I thought Janelle might want to see those."

"Yes." Anna swallowed. "There were some other photos, too. I think they might have been your other brother?"

His gray eyes locked on hers and Anna lost her breath for a moment. She tried to read what was in his expression—surprise? Embarrassment? Alarm?—but all she could see was the sea of gray sparked with silver and brown.

Grant nodded, then cleared his throat. "Since you failed to alert me in a timely fashion when my fly was down, I don't feel too bad about not noticing this earlier."

"Noticing what?"

"You've got frosting on your lip."

"What? Where?"

"Right here."

He reached out with a fingertip at the precise moment she licked her lower lip. She'd been aiming for the frosting, but got Grant instead.

The instant her tongue made contact with his finger, Grant groaned low in his throat. "God."

He started to draw his hand back, but Anna grabbed his wrist without thinking. She watched his pupils dilate, and the sight of all that blackness in a sea of gray made the heat coil deep in her belly.

Slowly, with aching deliberateness, she drew his finger into her mouth.

"Oh, Jesus, Anna."

She let the digit glide against the roof of her mouth, taking her time. Then she sucked him back in, stroking his fingertip with her tongue as she drew him deeper. She closed her eyes, savoring the taste of him, marveling at the size of his hand. His fingertip nearly reached the back of her throat, and she angled her head a little to take him in.

She slid her tongue over his knuckle and back around, sucking hard before releasing him again. Her grip was firm on his wrist, but he wasn't trying to pull away.

"Christ, you're so good with your mouth."

She smiled around his finger, drawing him in again, knowing he was picturing her mouth around his cock.

So was she.

She drew back, still holding fast to his wrist, and met his eyes.

"Want to see what else I can do with my mouth?"

• • •

Grant felt his gut clench at the boldness of her words. Or hell, maybe it was the thought of what she intended. Her mouth was inches from his fingertip, but that wasn't where he needed it to be.

She drew the tip of his finger into her mouth again, closing her eyes as Grant felt all the blood leave his brain. She released the pressure and drew back, then sucked him in again until he felt the tip of his finger touch the top of her throat. Her tongue was soft and warm and so goddamn wet as she slid back again and opened her eyes.

"Tell me what you want," she whispered.

Grant shifted his weight on the log, trying to ease the pressure of the hard-on straining against his fly. "You know what I want."

"Duh," she said, and somehow it was the single sexiest syllable he'd ever heard in his life. "The point is that I want to hear you say it."

"Anna, please —"

She laughed and wrapped her lips around his finger-tip, sliding her tongue around the length of the digit as she sucked him in again. The suction and the pressure and the warmth and the wetness was making him lose his mind.

"Anna, please —" He groaned again.

"Anna, please *what*?" she murmured, releasing his finger but not his wrist. "Say it, Grant. Come on. It does you no good to be the perfect, polite Boy Scout all the time. Tell me what you want me to do."

Her gaze locked on his, a challenge. Part of him wanted to get up and run from her, from this sensation, from the urge that told him to scrap all his gentlemanly inclinations and just order her down on her knees.

Most of him really liked the sound of that last bit.

He hesitated, then took a steadying breath.

"Suck my cock," he said. "Please," he added as an afterthought.

A slow grin spread across her face. "Well, since you're polite about it." She grinned wider. "Say it one more time. *Please*."

That last word sounded more like a taunt than a pleas-antry coming from those perfect, pink lips. But since he ur-gently wanted those perfect, pink lips wrapped around his shaft, he said it again.

"Suck me off, Anna. I want you and that perfect fucking mouth."

His voice was more forceful this time, and he watched her eyes flash with excitement. She licked her lips, and Grant felt his head begin to spin.

"My pleasure." She slid off the log and started to drop to

her knees. "Or yours."

"Wait."

He caught her by the arm with one hand and reached for his camera bag with the other. He yanked open the zipper and pulled out a small orange hand towel he kept there in case of unexpected downpours.

Or unexpected blowjobs. Whatever.

He spread it on the ground in front of him, kicking a small pebble out of the way. Anna laughed and dropped to her knees on the towel. "Always the gentleman."

She reached for his fly, and there was nothing gentlemanly about the way his cock surged against the front of his shorts. Anna slid her hand over his hard-on, stroking him through the fabric. She leaned forward and pressed her mouth to his fly, breathing hot breath through the twill until Grant heard himself groan.

"My, my, my," she murmured, sitting back on her heels as she stroked him through the fly of his shorts. "That's an impressive bulge you have there. Seems like it's just screaming to get out."

"Then do it." His words were more a growl than an actual sentence, and he couldn't believe the sound had come from him.

Anna grinned and gripped him harder. "Do what?"

"Take out my cock."

Her eyes flashed with desire again, and he wanted to flip her around and yank up her dress to have his way with her.

But Anna had other plans, and good manners dictated he should let her see those through.

"Take out your cock and do what?" she purred.

"Suck me. Hard. Please."

She laughed again and squeezed his balls through his shorts, making him ache with pleasure. Her nimble fingers undid the button at the top of his shorts, then dragged down the zipper with agonizing slowness. She wriggled her fingers through the fly of his boxer briefs. The instant her hand clenched around him, Grant felt all the air leave his body.

"Jesus," he hissed. "Yes."

Anna pulled his cock out through the fly, shoving the fabric back to expose him. The distant voices of the bridal party had vanished, and Grant hoped that was a good thing. At this point, he honest to God didn't care if the whole god-damn family showed up to take video.

Her mouth closed around the head of his erection, and Grant closed his eyes and moaned. She moved her tongue down the length of him, sucking him hard against the roof of her mouth. He'd never felt anything so warm and soft in his entire life, and he thought he might die from pleasure.

"Christ, Anna. That feels so fucking good."

Her eyes were closed, but he thought he saw the edges of her mouth curve into a smile. It was hard to tell with her hair falling in her eyes, all those luscious red-gold strands drifting across her flushed cheeks.

Grant reached down and threaded his fingers through her hair, pushing it back so he could see her beautiful face. She sucked him in deeper, and Grant felt his palms clench snug against her scalp. His fingers tangled tight in her hair, and he could feel the delicious rhythm of her head moving in his lap. She moaned and flicked her tongue over his shaft, opening her eyes to grin up at him.

"That's what I thought," she murmured, her breath hot on his thigh. "Beneath that Boy Scout facade, you're a filthy-talking, hair-pulling animal."

Grant blinked and started to unwind his fingers from her hair. But Anna reached up and grabbed his wrist, holding it in place. She turned her head to the side and bit his inner thigh. Hard.

"I like this side of you, Grant." She grinned up at him, her eyes sparking with fire. "The dark side. The side not everyone gets to see."

"I—"

"Show me the rest," she said and wrapped her lips around his cock again.

"Anna." He gasped, closing his eyes as she drew him into her mouth. "Your mouth is fucking magic. You make me so goddamn hard."

"Mmmm," she moaned against him, and the vibration damn near killed him. His brain was starting to buzz, and there was no blood left in his hands. Whether it was the tightness of her hair around his fingers or the tightness of her mouth around his shaft, he had no idea. He didn't care.

"Anna, you should stop."

"Mm-mm," she murmured around him, a moan or a refusal?

"Anna, I'm going to—"

His voice broke there, whether from the pressure of her tongue on his cock or a reluctance to say the words, he wasn't sure. She was sliding faster now, so hot and wet and tight and—

"Anna, Christ, you're going to make me come."

She dug her nails into his thighs, anchoring him there so that even if he wanted to pull back, he couldn't. Grant heard a strangled cry he realized was his own voice.

Sparks exploded in his brain and then from his fingertips and toes and every exposed inch of skin. He closed his eyes and gasped again as he surged and throbbed and pulsed hard and hot in her mouth.

When it was all over, Anna drew back and grinned at him. "That was fucking fantastic."

Grant gasped, too stunned and shell-shocked to move. "Holy hell."

She laughed. "I'll take that as a compliment."

"Can I get you some water or something?"

"Shut up, Grant."

There was no venom in her voice, and she was flushed and smiling as he slid his hands from her hair to cup her face. She blinked up at him with eyes so green he felt himself melt into them. "Jesus, you're beautiful," he choked out. "And amazing. And so fucking good at that I can't see straight."

She laughed and sat back on her heels. "Seeing you lose control like that? Hottest. Thing. Ever."

He dropped his hands from her face and shook his head. Reaching for his fly, he tucked himself back into his boxer briefs while Anna sat on her heels watching him. His breathing was almost back to normal, so he started to zip up, then decided it was more polite to help her up first. He held out his hand and she took it, her fingers small and warm in his.

He'd just begun to hoist her to her feet when she screamed.

Chapter Eight

The pain that radiated from Anna's right butt cheek was like nothing she'd felt before.

"What the fuck?" she screamed, rocketing to her feet like a hive of bees dipped in molten lava had just tunneled beneath her dress. Grant gripped her hand as she shrieked again, but all Anna wanted was to get away from the searing pain that speared her haunch.

"What is it? What happened?" His eyes were frantic as he scanned her for damage. Seeing her hand beneath her dress, he registered surprise. Then horror.

"Oh, shit." He looked down at the ground, kicked over a fallen palm frond, cursed again.

"Something stung me," Anna cried, still trying to figure out how she'd gone from post-blowjob bliss to brutal agony in five seconds.

Okay, maybe she was being a little dramatic. Still, it hurt like hell.

"A centipede." Grant stomped his foot on something, muttering as he stomped again. "Got it." He turned back to her, his brow furrowed and eyes wide with worry. "Let me scc."

Anna stopped rubbing her butt cheek and blinked at him. "I'm not flipping up my dress in the jungle."

"For crying out loud, Anna. Considering where your mouth was ten seconds ago, I think we're on familiar enough terms for me to see your butt."

Anna opened her mouth to say something sassy in retort, but another surge of stinging pain rocketed through her muscle and she cried out again. Grant grabbed her by the waist and flipped up the hem of her dress. She'd imagined exactly that scenario for the last thirty minutes, but this wasn't how she'd pictured it.

"Ouch!"

"Hold still, it's the right side?"

"Yes," she whimpered, wishing her voice didn't sound so pitiful.

"Thank God for thong panties. I can see the bite right there. Two little punctures like a snakebite."

"It's a bite? Not a sting?"

Grant let go of her and shook his head, his eyes scanning the ground around them. "Centipedes bite, or at least the ones on Hawaii do. It's very toxic and painful as hell."

"No kidding." Anna swallowed and tried to keep her hands from shaking. "Am I going to die?"

"No. It's not fatal. Not unless you have other medical issues like an allergy to bee stings?"

He was walking in circles, looking up at the treetops above them, then down at the ground again. Anna rubbed her butt and winced again.

"No allergies that I know of," she said.

"Good. Stay right here."

He dug into his camera bag and grabbed something, then sprinted to a spot about fifteen feet away. He stooped down, then turned and raced back to her gripping a papaya in one hand and a large knife in the other.

"What the hell?" she asked, not sure whether she meant the weapon or the fruit. "Is eating that supposed to help me?"

"No." Grant sliced into the papaya, his strokes even and lethal. Anna watched the juice dribble into the dirt at his feet and caught sight of something that looked like a pistol in his camera bag.

What kind of man brings an arsenal to a wedding?

A Patton man, she thought as she watched him hack into the flesh of the fruit. *A Marine.*

Grant dropped the knife on the ground, along with half the papaya. The other half was gripped in one hand as he reached for her with the other.

"Hold still," he commanded, catching her by the waist again. He flipped up the edge of her dress. "Move your hand."

She hadn't realized she was rubbing the bite mark until he said that. "I think you're taking this bossy thing a little far," she said, not wanting to admit she found it sexy as hell.

She didn't fool him, and he pushed her hand out of the way. "You like it," he said. "And also you need it. This will feel a little cold."

Before she could ask what he was doing, he was smooshing the papaya against her butt cheek in what was undoubtedly the weirdest postcoital activity she'd experienced.

"Aaah!" she cried out, noticing her voice sounded like a messed-up version of pleasure and pain. "What the—"

"The enzymes in the papaya will help digest the proteins in the centipede's venom and minimize the symptoms. Hold still and let me rub it in."

She could feel his fingertips massaging the area around the bite and tried not to imagine what she must look like with orangey goop smeared across her butt cheek. God, could this be any weirder?

"Is that helping at all?" he asked.

She nodded numbly, surprised to realize it did. And surprised to realize she was standing there in the jungle with a hot guy holding fruit on her ass.

"How do you know about this?"

"Jungle-warfare training. Also, I've spent a lot of time on Hawaii. Got bitten once myself. It hurts like a sonofabitch. You're being a real trooper."

Anna didn't feel like much of a trooper with her dress hoisted over her waist and fruit salad running down her leg, but she wasn't inclined to argue. She peered over her shoulder at Grant, who was eyeing her with concern.

He reached for her wrist, and for a moment she thought he was trying to hold her hand. Then she realized he was taking her pulse. "Are you feeling nauseous?" he asked.

"No."

"Headache?"

"No."

"Weakness? Heart palpitations?"

"A little, but I think that's because you keep touching my butt. Either that, or because I just gave you a blowjob in a tropical jungle. Not an everyday thing for me."

That got a smile out of him, albeit a small one. Grant was all business, and it was crazy how sexy she found that.

"How's the pain?"

"The papaya helps, but it still hurts like hell."

"Do you think you can make it to the hospital, or should I pee on you?"

"Pee on me?" Her shriek sent a flock of birds squawking from a nearby tree.

Grant nodded, looking stoic. "Urea and ammonia are basic urine compounds that neutralize the acidity of the poison. It'll help with pain and inflammation."

Anna shook her head, backing away. "No, thank you."

"Well you can't very well do it yourself."

"I'll stick with the papaya, thank you very—*ouch*!" She winced as another searing pain rippled through her. "Dammit, that hurts."

"It's working its way into your muscle. Come on, I'll drive you to the hospital. Can you hold this in place?"

Anna nodded and reached back to clutch the papaya in one shaky hand. She expected Grant to release his grip, but instead he moved his hand over hers and met her eyes with his. "I'm really sorry about this."

"It's okay. It's not like I'm going to die."

He shook his head. "I should have been more careful. I should have—"

"Known I might get my ass chewed by a bug with a hundred legs?" She shook he head. "No man thinks about that when he's getting a BJ."

"There's actually no such thing as a centipede with a hundred legs."

"What?"

He grimaced, looking almost regretful he'd said something so geeky. "Different species have varying numbers of legs, but they're always in odd-numbered pairs—you know, fifteen or seventeen pairs of legs, which means thirty or thirty-four individual legs."

She frowned at him. "Did you get your Boy Scout merit badge in entomology?"

"I enjoy reading zoology texts for fun."

"Of course you do. You can't just read a fucking *Playboy* magazine on the can like every other guy because you're fucking perfect."

Grant raised an eyebrow at her, clearly not seeing the connection. "You sure you're not feeling light-headed?"

"My head is perfectly fine," she said, trying not to love the feel of his massive hand covering hers while his other hand gently stroked her hip.

My heart, on the other hand—

"Ouch!" she said, wincing as pain gripped her again. She was pretty sure it was just the bite.

"Come on," he said, pressing the papaya more firmly against her flesh. "Let's get you to the hospital. You sure you don't want me to pee on you?"

"Um, what the hell?"

Anna turned at the sound of her sister's voice. From the edge of a clearing, Janelle emerged from behind a palm tree looking bemused.

Anna bit her lip. "I can explain."

Janelle raised an eyebrow, looking from Anna to Grant and back to Anna again. "You can explain why a strapping Marine is standing here with his fly undone offering to pee on you while he smears your ass with fruit?"

Anna winced and closed her eyes. "Maybe not."

• • •

By the time they left the hospital, Grant's nerves were shot. He looked over at Anna in the passenger seat and felt his heart lurch. She was curled with her feet under her and her hair falling around her face as she gazed out the window looking small and sleepy and vulnerable.

Not the first time someone got hurt because you couldn't keep your goddamn pants zipped. Way to go, asshole.

"Have you written your best man speech yet?"

Her words startled him so much he nearly drove off the road. He swerved a little, then overcorrected, his hands gripping the steering wheel so hard his knuckles were white. Anna turned away from the window to look at him.

Grant swallowed and tried to keep his face expressionless. "What was the question?"

"Your best man speech. For your sister's wedding next weekend? The best man usually gives a toast."

"Best man," Grant repeated, the words burning his tongue. "Right. I'm sure I'll come up with something."

She was studying him now, and Grant tried to keep his eyes on the road instead of on her. From the corner of his eye, he saw her shift in her seat, then wince.

He turned to look at her. "Are you in pain?"

"Surprisingly, not much. The pain meds are taking care of the bite just fine, but the seat belt just hit the spot where they gave me the tetanus shot. Who knew that would be mandatory?"

"I'm just glad you're feeling better. And I'm glad they

took extra precautions with you."

He didn't bother mentioning his role in that. He'd hovered around the waiting area like a nervous expectant dad, asking if they'd done tests to check for proteinuria or any indications of disintegrating skeletal muscle tissue or rhabdomyolysis—terms he knew zilch about, but had learned when he'd googled centipede bites on his iPhone. Holy shit, who knew there were so many horrible things that could happen to her?

"I still don't understand why they had to do an EKG," she said. "Do they normally do that for everyone who's bitten by a centipede on Hawaii?"

"Hard to say."

Hell, Grant could say. Of course they didn't, but he'd made such a nuisance of himself harassing the nurses about the possibility of abnormal muscle contractions in the heart and vapospasms leading to unwanted vasoconstriction— also shit he'd learned about while googling. The staff had finally agreed to test her for everything just to get rid of him.

Well, and because he handed over his AmEx card. That probably helped.

"Where are we going?" she asked.

"I'm taking a shortcut to get you back to your condo."

"Oh. Good." She sounded a little disappointed, but maybe she was just tired.

"I'll stick around to keep an eye on you. If you start developing a fever or necrosis or heart palpitations, I want to be there to help."

"That's very kind of you, but my sister—"

"Janelle went to go supervise the cleanup crew at the wedding reception. Then she said she needed to meet with the caterer for Sheri's wedding on the other side of the island."

"Dammit, that's right." Anna smacked her forehead with her hand. "I was supposed to do that tonight."

"Don't worry about it. Your sister has it covered. And I'll be looking out for you."

Anna looked out the window for a moment, quiet. When she turned back to him, there was a glint of something familiar in her eye. "Can we go back to your place instead of mine?"

"My place?"

"You have pie. The coconut-lime pie I brought you this morning? I hear it's a very good treatment for centipede bites. Even better than smearing me with papaya."

Grant laughed and nodded. "Sure."

That was just as well. His house was closer to the hospital than the condo where she and Janelle were staying, plus he had a first-aid kit in his medicine cabinet with plenty of antibiotic ointment.

That's not why you want to get her back to your place.

"I'm sorry again about what happened," he said.

"Quit saying that," she said. "It's not your fault. It hardly even hurts anymore. Besides, it was kinda worth it."

He glanced over to see her grinning at him, and he couldn't help but smile in return. "Doesn't seem fair I got all the pleasure and you got all the pain."

"Au contraire," she said, licking her lips. "That was the most pleasure I've had in a long time. Seeing your perfect, gentlemanly exterior crack wide open to reveal the sex beast beneath? I think I had an orgasm just witnessing that."

The thought of her having an orgasm made Grant nearly

drive off the road again. Christ, at the rate he was going, she probably thought he was drunk. He hit his turn signal and slowed down to take the corner toward his house. "Well thank you very much for the—"

He stopped, not sure what the etiquette called for here. Anna was looking at him with a bemused expression.

"Blowjob? Hummer? Blumpkin? Knobjob?"

"Right."

She laughed. "Anytime, Boy Scout."

He tried not to read too much into that as he parked the car in the driveway, then ran around to open her door and help her out. She didn't argue, which probably said something. If she was willing to let him baby her a little, she must still be hurting.

Grant led her up the walk and unlocked the front door, ushering her inside. "Do you want to sit inside or outside on the lanai?"

"How about inside? That sofa looks comfortable, and I think I've had enough of the great outdoors today."

"Janelle said the same thing at the hospital. Actually, I think her exact words were, 'Fuck the great outdoors, where's the nearest spa?'"

Anna laughed. "That sounds like my sister."

"I take it you girls are more the indoorsy type?"

"Janelle more than me," she said, easing herself onto the sofa. Grant handed her an afghan knitted by his mom when he was still in diapers. A silly gesture, since it was seventy degrees in his house, but Anna took it without comment.

"I think I already mentioned my sister is the consummate city slicker," she continued, curling up with her right hip eased up off the sofa. "I'm surprised she even agreed to come on this trip, what with there being no skyscrapers or bagel shops near our condo."

"Hawaii's not her scene?" he asked, tearing his eyes away from the lovely curve of her hip to hustle into the kitchen. He pulled the pie out of the fridge and glanced over his shoulder to see her balled up on the sofa with her feet tucked under her looking small and tired. Grant felt his gut twist. He sliced an extra large piece for her, arranging it on a blue plate his sister had given him the last time she'd cleaned out her cupboards. He sliced himself a piece, too, and grabbed two forks from the drawer.

"Hawaii isn't really Janelle's scene, though it's definitely more palatable than, say, a deserted mountain cabin in the woods," Anna said. "I think this trip was just a good excuse for her to be far away from her ex-husband for a little while."

Grant returned to the living room with the two pie plates. He handed one to Anna and sat down beside her. "Was he abusive?"

Anna seemed to hesitate, and he wondered if she was protecting her sister or just choosing her words carefully. "Janelle was very selective about the details she shared from her marriage. I don't think he hit her, but I do think he was emotionally abusive. He cheated on her, but that wasn't all of it. I can't put my finger on it, but there was always something off about him."

"Like what?"

"I'm not sure. Like he had secrets, maybe. Besides the affair, I mean. Something he was up to that none of us knew about. He was very controlling with Janelle. He used to listen to her phone messages, demand to know where she was every minute of the day, sometimes even had her watched."

Grant frowned. "Those sound like signs of abuse." He watched a flash of regret cross her face and wished he'd chosen his words more carefully.

"I hope not," she said softly. "He seemed like a nice enough guy when she introduced me, and then I got so wrapped up in planning their wedding that—" She frowned, looking down at her pie. "Maybe I missed something."

"You couldn't have known."

"That's just it—I *should* have. I was clueless about the problems in my parents' marriage as a kid, and then I failed to see everything wrong with Janelle's husband when he was standing right in front of me picking out cummerbunds and honeymoon destinations." She laughed, but it was a dry and bitter sound. "Christ, I didn't even notice Mac and Kelli's engagement was a sham. How clueless can one person be?"

He looked at her carefully, knowing it was important not to say the wrong thing here. "Anyone with eyes could look at Mac and Kelli and know they were in love. They were the only two people on earth who didn't notice."

"Still, it's a pattern. Don't you see? With that many strikes against me when it comes to judging relationships and character, I shouldn't be allowed to pick out my own toothbrush, let alone a life partner."

"Anna, none of that is your fault. Your parents, your sister—they made their own decisions. You can't go around penalizing yourself for other people's relationship missteps. You're not to blame here."

She looked at him over a forkful of pie. "This from the guy who won't stop blaming himself for my centipede bite."

Grant frowned, not sure how they'd gone from talking about her issues to his. He sensed there was more to her story, something she wasn't telling him yet. He wanted to push, but he needed to redirect the conversation onto safer turf. "Are you doing okay? You need me to get you some pain pills or some water or anything?"

"I'm fine, Grant. She looked at him oddly, slicing the side of her fork through her hunk of pie. "How about we both agree to make an effort to stop blaming ourselves for shitty things that happened to other people?"

Grant swallowed a mouthful of pie, trying to get it past the lump that had formed in his throat. She was getting too close for comfort here, so he nodded at her plate. "Sure thing. What's in this anyway? Did you really make that with the coconut that hit me on the head?"

She looked down at the pie, then back at him, tilting her head to the side a little. "It's good, huh? Coconut and lime juice are the main ingredients, but there are macadamia nuts in the crust."

"It's amazing."

She was studying him in earnest, probably aware that he'd just changed the subject, but she didn't say anything. The silence stretched between them for a little while, but Grant didn't rush to fill it. Let her do the talking.

"I still can't believe my sister found you rubbing papaya on my butt with your fly down," she said at last. "What are the odds?"

"Apparently slightly better than the odds of her showing up five minutes earlier and finding us in a much more compromising position."

"Good point." Anna set her fork on her empty plate and pushed the plate aside on the end table. "That wasn't nearly as embarrassing as the time Janelle and I were both in middle school and had a crush on the same boy. She was in sixth grade and I was in eighth, but the boy was a seventh grader. Fair game for us both, right?"

"All's fair in love and war and junior high."

"Exactly. So anyway, we were at this school party hoping the boy would ask us to dance instead of sitting on the far side of the gym making paper airplanes with his buddies."

Grant grinned, remembering how he and Schwartz used to do the same damn thing before they discovered girls a year or two later. "Seventh grade boys are not known for their romantic prowess and emotional perception."

She laughed. "I'm not sure they change much even with fifteen or twenty years of experience. Anyway, I suddenly got a migraine. I ran to the bathroom thinking I could stay there in the quiet with the lights out and maybe it would go away. I also had to pee, so I was sitting there with my Hello Kitty underpants around my knees, when all of a sudden I felt nauseous."

"Oh, no."

"Oh, yes. I threw up all over my underwear. My favorite ones."

Grant grimaced, though he secretly felt a little flattered she was open enough to tell him such an unflattering story. "What did you do?"

She rolled her eyes and shifted position on the couch. "While the idea of going commando can be sexy and titillating at age twenty-seven, it's the most horrifying idea in the world for a twelve-year-old girl wearing her prettiest, shortest, pink skirt."

"I can imagine."

"I sat there and cried for awhile. Eventually, Janelle

came in and found me."

"Uh-oh." Grant took his last bite of pie and set the plate aside, trying not to feel horribly sorry for twelve-year-old Anna in her state of despair. "Don't tell me she went back out and told the boy?"

Anna shook her head and smiled. "Definitely not. She helped me clean up the mess and gave me her sweatshirt to wrap around my waist. Then she called our mom to come get us and led me out the side door so we could wait for her to give us a ride home."

"She left the party, too?"

"Yep. Neither one of us got to dance with the boy. Eventually, I heard he grew up and married a guy he met at the dance that night. They're living happily in Seattle with two kids and a potbellied pig."

Grant laughed. "Sounds like a good happily ever after for all involved."

"Pretty much," Anna said, but her expression was a little wistful. She twisted her hands up in the afghan. "So how about you?"

"What about me?"

"Got any good stories? Embarrassing ones or sibling stories, take your pick. Or both. That works, too."

Grant thought about it a minute. What was he willing to reveal to her?

He thought about childhood antics with his brothers, he and Schwartz pantsing each other and learning to make armpit farts while Mac looked on with stoic irritation. He thought about his first year in college when Schwartz saved his ass at a frat party when he fell out a window throwing water balloons and needed six stitches on his forehead. He thought about the stupid mistake he'd made that night at the bar in California—

He clamped his brain down tight on that line of thinking. He didn't want to share any of that.

You'll bare your junk to this woman, but not your soul?

Grant cleared his throat and shrugged. "I had some leave a few months ago and did a surf trip with some buddies in Mexico."

"That's right, you visited Mac and Kelli the same time I did. I can't believe we never crossed paths."

"It's too bad," he said, trying not to picture himself twined in a hammock with a bikini-clad Anna, tipsy on tequila and Mexican sunshine. "Anyway, I took a little Spanish in college, so I was trying to show off one night after I walked into the ladies' room by mistake. I told the bartender I felt *embarazada*. Embarrassed, right?"

"Sure, that makes sense."

"Only it doesn't. Embarrassed in Spanish is *vergüenza*. *Embarazada* means pregnant."

Anna burst out laughing, and Grant laughed along with her. He loved the way her eyes lit up and how she threw her head back, exposing the pale column of her throat. He thought about planting a trail of kisses from the hollow right below her chin and leading down her sternum, over her collarbones, peeling back the lacy cup of her bra, and—

"Grant?"

"What?"

"Why are you looking at me like that?"

"Like what?"

She folded her arms over her chest, a gesture that made her small breasts press together high and soft and round in the scooped neckline of her dress. Grant ached to slide his tongue into that perfect hollow between them, but Anna was talking again.

"Two days ago I would have mistaken that look for the politely attentive expression of a man engaged in friendly conversation." Her eyes were locked on his in a familiar dare he'd begun to recognize. "But now that I know there's a deliciously filthy-mouthed sex machine lurking under your Boy Scout exterior, I'm inclined to think that's the look of a man having dirty thoughts."

Grant swallowed and considered arguing. But hell, she'd called him out fair and square. What did he have to lose?

"I can't fault your powers of observation," he said slowly. "Or your bluntness."

She grinned and wriggled her feet forward on the sofa, tucking them under his thigh. "You keep saying that—how you admire my blunt nature—but you could do it, too, you know."

"Be blunt?" He shook his head. "Not my style."

"Sure it is. You just need practice."

"Practice?"

"Yes. I notice you pause a little bit before you say anything. Like you're thinking about what you really want to say, then editing it to give a response you think is more appropriate. It's endearing, really, but that's gotta get old for you."

Grant thought about it for a minute. It wasn't easy, since he kept getting distracted by the warmth of her bare toes beneath his thigh and by the fact that the angle of her knees gave him a view that almost went straight up her dress. If she'd just move her ankle to one side—

"I have an idea!" she said, jumping up so fast Grant nearly fell over. "We're going to give you a little bluntness training."

"Bluntness training?" he echoed, already missing the feel of her shins pressed warmly against his leg and the sight of her bare thigh barely concealed beneath the hem of her dress.

"Yes," she said, dragging one of his dining room chairs over to a spot beside his stove. He watched her climb up on it and stood up to catch her in case she toppled.

"Anna, what on earth—"

"Got it!" she said, wrestling the nine-volt battery out of the smoke detector. She jumped off the chair and padded back toward the sofa, leaving Grant to stare mutely after her. "I promise I'll put it back in just a few minutes."

"What are you—"

"Get ready, Boy Scout. I'm going to need your tongue."

Chapter Nine

This is probably a really dumb idea, Anna thought as she dropped onto the sofa beside Grant. The pain in her butt was totally gone, replaced by something warm and tingly that probably had nothing to do with the drugs they'd offered at the hospital.

Grant was looking at her like he suspected her pain meds were making her loopy, which was possible. But it was also possible she just wanted to have a little fun with this guy while she could. Breaking through his Boy Scout facade to reveal his inner sex beast earlier had been hot as hell. She kinda wanted to see it again if she could.

Besides, she had a hunch there was more to Grant Patton than he let anyone else see. Something behind his careful veil of perfection. Maybe this was a way to peek behind it.

"Okay, we're going to do a homemade lie detector test," she said, tucking her bare feet beneath his thigh again and pressing her knees together so she didn't give him an inadvertent peep show. "One that involves some mild electrocution."

Grant raised an eyebrow and stared at the battery in her hand. "I've used polygraphs before in counterintelligence work. I don't recall anything about electrocution." He frowned. "Or tongues. Why did you say you needed mine?"

"Patience, Boy Scout. We'll get to that. First, tell me some of the physical signs that someone's lying or talking about something that makes him uncomfortable."

"Increased heart rate," Grant said automatically. "Fidgeting. Failure to make eye contact. Dilated pupils, rapid breathing, sweating."

"Okay, good. I'm going to ask you some questions. If I see you hesitate or I think you're not being totally honest about your answer, you have to lick the battery."

"Lick the battery?"

"Didn't you do this as a kid?" She turned the battery over in her hand, tapping the end with the tip of her finger. "You touch your tongue to the two contact points on a nine-volt battery and it gives you a mild shock. Not enough to kill you, or even hurt that badly. It's just a jolt. I'm not totally sure how it works, but it seems like a good deterrent against fibbing and half-truths, don't you think?"

He was staring at her with an incredulous expression, but there was amusement in his eyes. "Did the doctor say anything about centipede venom getting into your brain?"

"Come on, Grant. It'll be fun."

"Electrocution usually is. You're aware that since I'm trained in recognizing the signs of lying, I'm also trained at disguising them in myself."

"Sure, but why would you? The point is that we're training

you to speak your mind. To be blunt, which is something you want to work on. What's the point in faking it?"

He seemed to consider that a moment, then nodded. "Fair enough. So how about positive reinforcement?"

She wiggled her toes beneath his thigh. "What did you have in mind?"

"Some sort of reward system. For when I reply with the requisite amount of bluntness, of course."

"That sounds fair. What do you want?"

"It'll depend on the question, I suppose."

The predatory gleam in his eye was enough to leave her squirming in her seat, but she nodded. "We'll cross that bridge when we come to it. Okay, first question." She thought about it a moment, trying to come up with something simple but not too simple. "What's the last dirty thought you had?"

He hesitated a moment. His hands were clasped in his lap like he was working hard to keep them to himself. At last he nodded toward the front of her dress. "I thought about licking that little hollow spot between your breasts."

A shudder of pleasure arced through her, but Anna forced herself to nod impassively. "You hesitated a little on that one, but I'm going to give you the benefit of the doubt since your answer was good. No punishment necessary." She clenched the battery in her fist and wriggled her toes under his thigh again, loving the solidness and warmth of his body touching hers.

"And my reward?"

"What would you like?"

"A kiss."

She raised an eyebrow at him, which seemed a more suitable response than climbing into his lap. "I thought we decided to keep things professional between us since we're working together and all."

"That pretty much went out the window the second you got on your knees and ordered me to talk dirty. Kiss me, Anna."

He didn't wait for her to come to him. He unclasped his hands and slid one around the back of her head, pulling her against him. His lips touched hers, and Anna held her breath, waiting to see if this would be an innocent peck or something more.

There was nothing innocent about it. The kiss was long and slow and deep, and by the time it ended, Anna was seeing pinpricks of light in her peripheral vision.

"Okay," she said, a little breathless as she scooted back on the sofa. Lord, the man could kiss. Anna swallowed. "Next question. Does my sister have better boobs than I do?"

"No."

His response was so forceful and automatic that Anna sat back a little. He was either completely sincere, or smart enough to know better than to answer honestly.

"She's got a full cup size on me," Anna pointed out.

"Size isn't everything. Yours are perkier and have a nicer shape. They've got more dimension around the sides, more fullness through here. Plus they look spectacular when you ditch the bra, which is something bustier women seldom do."

Anna blinked, taken aback. "You've spent a lot of time studying breasts."

"What man hasn't?"

"Studying *my* breasts."

"What man wouldn't?" He reached for her again. "I'll take another kiss now."

His lips were on hers before she could protest—not that she planned to. His mouth was warm and soft and so god-damn good at what it was doing. His palm slid up her back this time, then veered to the side to graze the edge of her breast. Anna shuddered under his touch, urging him to keep sliding, to cup her breast in his palm.

When he released her this time, every inch of Anna's body was tingling. Grant held her gaze, looking deliciously smug.

Anna licked her lips. "Let's try a tougher one now. Give me one piece of constructive criticism on my fellatio technique."

Grant snorted. "No."

"Afraid I can't take it? Come on, surely there's room for improvement somewhere. Maybe a little more suction or some hand work or—"

"No," he repeated, more forceful this time. "There's not a damn thing I'd change about the way you—" He cut off there, and she watched his Adam's apple move as he swallowed, fishing for the right word. "Performed," he added at last.

"Lick the battery," she said, holding it out to him.

"What the hell for? I didn't lie."

"Maybe, maybe not. But you did hesitate to say the word blowjob, so that violates the rules of bluntness training."

Grant rolled his eyes. "Do I get to see this rule book at some point?"

"Lick it," she said, thrusting the battery at him again.

He started to argue, then shrugged. "I make it a policy never to say no to a woman who issues an order like that."

He leaned forward, not hesitating even a little the way

she and Janelle used to as little kids daring each other, "Do it!" then "No, *you* do it." He wrapped his hand around hers, holding it steady as he stuck out his tongue and touched it to the contact points on the battery.

Grant didn't flinch.

He drew back and nodded at her. "There you go."

She frowned down at the battery. "Is this thing dead?"

"No."

"Did you get a jolt?"

"Go on. You try it."

She lowered her tongue to the metallic prongs. A metallic zap coursed through her mouth, and she jerked her head back. "Yeowch!"

He grinned. "Guess I don't need to replace the battery in my smoke detector. You'll have to come over every few months and check it with your tongue. I'll take my reward now."

"Your reward?"

"This," he said, capturing the hand that wasn't holding the battery. Before she knew what was happening, he'd drawn her hand to his mouth. His breath was warm on her palm as he uncurled her fingers and slipped his tongue into the junction between her index and middle finger. He stroked the webbing between the digits with such aching softness, Anna moaned aloud. He continued to lick her there, teasing the delicate skin with a few more strokes as he gripped her wrist with one hand. At last, he released her.

Anna sat back, pulse pounding in her ears, nerves screaming between her legs. Grant held her gaze, unblinking.

"You're not the only one who can do oral innuendo," he said.

"No kidding," she murmured, staring at his mouth. She wanted it everywhere. Well, a few places in particular.

Instead, she cleared her throat. "Okay, next question. Ever cheated on a girlfriend?"

Something dark flashed in his eyes. It was gone in an instant, and she might have imagined it entirely.

But something told her she hadn't.

"No," Grant said, his voice firm.

She reached for his wrist and pressed two fingers against his pulse. Steady, not too quick, though what the hell did she know about his normal heart rate? She touched a hand to his face, trying to ascertain whether he was warm or sweaty, but hell, it was a warm day in Hawaii. Who wasn't sweaty?

"Dilated pupils are also a sign of arousal," he said, causing her to drop her hand from his face. "In case you planned to ding me for that."

"Next question," she said, pretty sure there was something more there, but not wanting to dwell on it or bother with the punishment or reward. Part of her wanted to ask about the brother in the photos. About why she'd never heard more about him, and why Grant had such a haunted-looking photograph of the man.

But something stopped her. Something made her bite her lip, then opt for a softball.

"Name something your mother cooks for family dinners that you pretend to like because you want to be polite but secretly you can't stand it."

"Brussel sprouts," he said. "And lima beans. And shit-on-a-shingle."

"Your mother serves you something called shit-on-a-shingle?"

"My mother flies fighter jets and knows how to operate a grenade launcher," Grant replied, his voice tinged with pride. "She didn't spend my childhood making cutesy-sounding recipes from *Better Homes and Gardens*."

Anna grinned. "Your mom is awesome. She wore a shoulder holster to my first wedding planning meeting with your sister and Sam. You get a pass on that one." She flipped the battery over in her fingers, trying to think of something she knew might make him uncomfortable. A subject that had made him uncomfortable before.

She stopped fiddling with the battery and looked at him. "Why don't you want to be the best man in your sister's wedding?"

"I don't like standing up in front of crowds."

There was no hesitation in his answer, no physical signs of discomfort. Still, she knew he was lying. She could sense it.

What else was he hiding?

"When you're doing your spy-catcher work, do you sometimes know someone's lying even though you can't prove it?"

"All the time."

She nodded. "You either need to lick the battery on the best man question, or tell me the real reason."

He stared at the battery in her hand a moment, then met her eyes. "I'd like to lick it."

His voice was so molten, so suggestive, she almost forgot she needed to press harder to get the answer. To dig a little deeper. There was something there, she knew it, but the tip of his tongue grazing the top of the battery was enough to send her thoughts skewing in a different direction. They could come back to that later.

Grant sat back and stared at her. His pupils were inky and his expression was so predatory she shivered. "Any more questions?"

Anna licked her lips. "Just one."

"What's that?"

She swallowed, taking a moment to consider her words. They'd agreed to keep things professional, but weren't they well beyond that now? How much did it really matter, anyway?

Anna took a steadying breath. "Do you want to fuck me?"

"No."

"No?" A wave of disappointment sloshed in her belly, but she tried not to let it show on her face.

Grant slid his hand over her knee, claiming it, as his gaze held hers. "Right now, I don't want to fuck you. What I want to do is make love to you so fiercely you forget your own name."

Anna dropped the battery. She felt it thunk against her anklebone, and it probably hurt, but she didn't feel a damn thing. She couldn't breathe. She couldn't blink. All she could do was stare into those gray eyes and nod.

"Okay."

Her acquiescence was probably irrelevant at this point. Not that Grant was the sort of guy to take her without consent, but with every nerve in her body screaming consent in a shrieking harmony of hormones, it was pretty damn obvious she wanted him.

He stood up and moved his hands under her. Before she could ask what he was doing, he'd scooped her into his arms and was carrying her down the hallway toward his bedroom.

"Grant, I can walk."

"Of course you can. I'd just prefer to carry you at this moment."

His chest was huge and muscular, and his arms were flexed with the effort of holding her. She knew this sort of caveman behavior shouldn't turn her on, but she was so wet from wanting him that her thighs felt glued together.

He turned the corner and took four steps to the bed. He tossed her backward, and she flailed for a moment, struggling for a graceful landing. Grant was on her in an instant, his eyes locked with hers as he grabbed the hem of her dress and tugged it upward. She raised her arms like an obedient girl, breathless with heat and the sheer power of him. He flung her dress aside and claimed her mouth, kissing her with a ferocity that left her moaning against his lips.

When he drew back, his eyes were molten. "I want to make you come until you can't stand."

She could only nod as he reached for the waistband of her panties. She wasn't wearing a bra—thank God for that— and he stripped the lacy thong from her and grabbed her legs. Shoving her thighs apart, he sank to his knees beside the bed. He caught her by the hips and pulled her roughly to the edge of the mattress.

For an instant, she felt exposed. Vulnerable. Naked. Then his mouth was on her and she forgot all that, forgot her insecurities and her self-consciousness and probably her social security number as his tongue plunged into her.

"Oh, God!" she cried out, clenching her fingers in his hair as she arched her hips up.

He responded by pushing her thighs open wider, his mouth everywhere at once as he licked and stroked and devoured her. He slid one finger into her, then two, and holy mother of hell what was that spot he grazed with his fingertip? It felt so goddamn good in places she never knew she had and if he didn't stop stroking like that, she was seriously going to—

"I'm going to come."

"Mmm," he murmured against her, and the vibration was enough to send her skyrocketing to oblivion. She shrieked as the first wave of orgasm hit her, then another, and too many more to count. He rode it with her, probing, stroking, licking, making her mindless until she was panting and breathless on the damp duvet.

When she opened her eyes, he was hovering over her. His gaze locked with hers, hot and gray and molten. "You are delicious."

"You are—" She tried to recall if she needed an adjective or a noun or a verb, but couldn't remember what any of those things were anyway, so it didn't matter. "Holy fuck."

He grinned and reached behind him to the nightstand. She heard the crinkle of cellophane and knew he was slipping on a condom. Somehow he managed to do it without breaking eye contact, without taking his hand off her hip. He moved over her, strong, forceful, intense.

She felt his knee between hers, pushing her legs apart. The weight of him on top of her was exquisite, the points of his hip bones hard against her softness. She opened her legs wider and pressed the heels of her hands against his ass. His eyes were still locked on hers, and though he hadn't said a word, she nodded.

"Yes."

Grant slid into her and Anna gasped, shocked at how

deeply he filled her. His forehead was inches from hers, those gray eyes drilling into her as he drew back and plunged into her again. She closed her eyes and cried out, stunned by the magnitude of the sensation. Even with her eyes shut tight, she could feel his gaze on hers.

"Anna," he murmured and drove into her again.

His rhythm was achingly slow, and Anna arched up to meet his thrust. She opened her eyes again and lost herself in the gray depths of his. She could see every fleck of silver, every warm hint of taupe, a kaleidoscope of ash and earth and sky and cloud in that intense gaze.

She was breathing fast now, and realized he was matching her breath for breath, thrust for thrust. He drove into her again, and Anna lifted her hips to feel him deeper.

He angled up on his forearms, rising above her as he thrust into her at an angle that made her cry out again. She could see every ripple of muscle in his chest, the hugeness of his biceps, the span of his shoulders, and still, those eyes, *those eyes—*

"My God," she whimpered, fingers clenching so hard in the sheets she felt her fingernail split. There was something about the eye contact that amplified every thrust, every breath, every pulse, every point where their skin touched.

Something was buzzing in the back of her brain, faint at first, then louder until her ears roared with sound and sensation. She could feel herself hurtling toward the edge, and she raised her hips to meet it.

"Grant," she gasped.

A knowing look flashed in his eyes as he drove into her harder, his forehead nearly touching hers, their gazes locked as tightly as their bodies as Anna cried out and clenched her thighs around him.

"That's it," he whispered, thrusting deep as something inside her exploded. "Let go."

She did, giving in to an eruption of pleasure that pulsed through her whole body.

Grant was two beats behind. "Oh, God."

She saw it in his eyes the instant he toppled into the chasm with her. A momentary flash of surprise, then pleasure so intense his eyes went dark with it. Anna screamed and clawed his back, but Grant didn't flinch. He drove into her again as Anna arched and bucked and cried out, his eyes never leaving hers.

At last, she felt him go still. Anna was the first to blink.

"What the hell was that?"

Grant laughed and rolled to the side, pulling her with him. "I'm not sure whether to take that as a compliment or a sign of medical distress."

His hand slid over her waist, and Anna let him pull her up so they lay face-to-face, nose to nose, chest to chest. She breathed him in, still too shell-shocked to do anything but stare at him.

"That thing you did with the intense eye contact and the breathing and your hips and—" She stopped, not sure she was making any sense or that he was even aware of any of the things he'd done to blow her mind. She swallowed and reached a hand up to stroke the side of his face. "That was amazing."

He grinned. "It was. Thank you."

She opened her mouth to say more, then shut it. She honestly wasn't sure what words might come tumbling out, and some things were better left unsaid.

Instead, she settled for snuggling closer to his chest and closing her eyes. "You feel good."

He planted a kiss at the edge of her hairline, and she felt him draw a breath as he did it. "Are you tired? I know some of those meds can make you drowsy."

"I'm fine," she murmured, though her limbs were already feeling heavy with fatigue.

"Does the bite hurt?"

"Not at all. Sex is the world's best painkiller."

"You can stay here tonight if you want. I'll call Janelle to let her know."

"Mmmm," Anna replied, not sure how she'd gotten so tired all of a sudden but knowing it was useless to fight. She could trust Grant to take care of things. Hell, she could trust him to repave her driveway if she needed it. He was the kind of man a woman could count on as a friend, a lover, a husband—

She stopped, wide awake now. *Husband?*

She swallowed hard, curling her body against his. "Grant?"

"Mmmhm?"

"There's something I feel like I should tell you."

"Should I get the battery?"

She laughed, but it came out sounding stilted and nervous. "I don't need the battery, but I do need to swear you to secrecy."

His palm curled around her hip, and he drew her closer. "What is it?"

She sighed and reached down to grip his hand. "It's something I've never told anyone else before," she said, her voice soft and shaky. "Something I want to tell *you*."

Chapter Ten

Anna swallowed hard, gathering the nerve to confess her darkest secret. Beside her, Grant angled up on one elbow to peer down at her.

"What is it?" he asked, his voice tinged with concern as those storm-gray eyes looked into hers.

"It's about marriage. I've only told you half the truth about why I don't want to get married. *Ever*," she added, in case he'd forgotten.

"Did something happen?"

"I guess you could say that," she said, closing her eyes so she wouldn't feel his boring into her soul. "I was serious about Janelle's divorce being my last straw, the final thing that convinced me I can't trust my judgment when it comes to relationships. But something happened about a year before that. It was part of the reason I pushed so hard for Janelle to marry Jacques. I wanted someone in our family to finally get it right."

Grant's breath was soft and warm against her skin. "How do you mean?"

"I met this guy at my favorite lunch spot in Portland. We both ordered the green curry with chicken and our orders got mixed up and—anyway, it doesn't matter. It seemed like a sign. Like fate."

"Fate," he repeated, and Anna opened her eyes. She half expected to see judgment or mockery in his expression, but all she saw was encouragement. She took a shaky breath and kept going.

"It was a whirlwind romance. We hung out together for three days straight, sharing secrets and family stories and cheap pizza. That Friday night, we were both a little tipsy on red wine. I made a joke about flying to Vegas and getting married, and he just looked at me and said, 'Let's do it.'"

"What?"

Anna nodded. "I know it sounds stupid, but I was caught up in the romance of it all. I had a couple flight vouchers a client had given me, and that seemed like a sign, too. My house is a ten-minute cab ride from the airport, and it takes less than two hours to fly from Portland to Las Vegas. Before I had a chance to blink, we were standing in a cheesy Elvis-themed chapel getting ready to walk down the aisle."

Grant lifted a hand and brushed her hair off her forehead, his eyes soft as they held hers. "Did you go through with it?"

"No. Just as we got in line for the paperwork, he chickened out. Said he couldn't marry me because he was already married." She choked out a little laugh that ended up sounding more like a sob. "*Already married.* Can you believe it?"

Grant planted another kiss along her hairline. "Sounds like you dodged a bullet. Do you still love him?"

"No," she said, tracing a finger over a thin stripe of satin on the edge of the sheet. "I didn't love him to begin with. I barely remember his name. I was just wrapped up in the passion of it all, of the idea that fate had brought us together and the whole thing was meant to be. If it weren't for the small detail of bigamy being illegal, I would have pledged eternal devotion to a guy I barely knew."

He was quiet a minute, digesting the information. She looked down at the sheet covering her breasts, wondering what Grant must think of her.

"We all make mistakes, Anna," he murmured, stroking his hand down her shoulder. "We all do stupid things we regret."

Something in his voice made her meet his eyes again. There was a flash of guilt, a flicker of something that told her he knew plenty about regret.

She sighed. "I know, but don't you see? I had a hand in wrecking my parents' marriage. I pushed my sister to marry a guy who turned out to be an emotionally abusive philanderer. I couldn't even tell when my own friend, Kelli, hired me to plan a fake wedding for her fake engagement. But this—" She waved a hand, hoping he understood she meant her own near miss marriage instead of anything that had transpired in this bedroom. "It's inexcusable, Grant. It's irrefutable proof that I lack the good judgment to ever make a permanent commitment to anyone."

He was quiet a moment, and Anna took another breath. She wouldn't blame him for thinking she was ridiculous. What sort of woman ran off to Vegas to marry a total stranger? A stranger who turned out to be married already. For crying out loud—

"Anna?"

"Yeah?"

"You've never told anyone that story before?"

She shook her head and looked back down at the sheet. "Never."

"Why me?"

"I don't know. I guess because we'd been talking about marriage. About our reasons for never wanting to do it. I felt like I owed you the full truth."

He nodded. "Thank you."

She met his eyes again. "You don't think I'm an idiot?"

"On the contrary. I think you're a beautiful, creative, intelligent woman with an amazing capacity for passion."

She shook her head, not convinced. "But you see now why I don't want to get married? Why that's not something I can ever bring myself to do."

"Hey, I'm the last guy in the world to try to talk you into marriage, but I can tell you this," he said, sliding his palm down her rib cage to cup her hip. "You're human. And you learn from your mistakes. That's a pretty admirable thing."

"But they're pretty serious mistakes to make. And I've been so embarrassed about the stupid Vegas thing."

"We don't ever have to talk about it again," he murmured, kissing the tip of her ear. "I'm just honored you told me."

She raised an eyebrow at him. "You're sure you don't want to laugh at me just a little?"

"Not one bit."

"But—"

"Shhh," he said, planting a kiss on the tip of her nose. "You don't owe me any more explanations. I don't think less of you. I admire the hell out of your honesty."

"Oh." She blinked up at him, suddenly more exhausted than she'd ever been in her life. "I'm having trouble keeping my eyes open."

"Those meds they gave you are pretty strong."

She smiled. "Painkillers and amazing sex. A winning combination."

"Go to sleep. I'll call Janelle and tell her everything." He squeezed her thigh beneath the sheet. "About you staying over, I mean. The rest of your secrets are safe with me."

"Thank you." Her eyelids were unbearably heavy, so she let them fall shut. She burrowed against him, feeling safer and warmer than she had in years. "It felt really good to get that off my chest."

He was quiet beside her, and she thought maybe he was drifting off, too. When he spoke, his voice sounded far away.

"I can only imagine," he murmured, pulling her tight against him.

• • •

Grant awoke at sunrise like he always did. He opened his eyes and looked at the clock the way he did every morning, confirming it was a little before six a.m. like it was every day when he popped awake with a lengthy to do list and a raging case of morning wood.

He rolled over and found his feet tangled with a smaller, softer pair, and it took him a moment to remember everything that had happened.

Not the typical morning. Not by a long shot.

Anna.

God. How the hell had he gotten in so deep? He'd seen

the look in her eye the instant she shattered beneath him. He'd felt the crackle of electricity, the arc of connection he swore he'd never allow to happen. And he'd felt the bond cinch tighter the moment she confessed her secret.

Her story hadn't bothered him a bit. If anything, it made him adore her more, made him admire her passion and her honesty.

That's the scariest thought you could have.

Grant closed his eyes a moment, summoning the strength to leave. Then he rolled out of bed and made his way down the hall, pulling on a pair of gym shorts as he blinked in the half-light of early morning.

He set up the coffeemaker for her so all she had to do was press a button. He wrote a quick note about it, ending with a platitude about how he hoped she slept well and thanking her for last night.

He stared at the note for a moment, then anchored it on the counter beneath a coffee mug so she'd be sure to see it. Then he walked out beneath the plumeria tree in the front yard and plucked one of the fragrant blooms from a low branch. He brought it back inside and set it beside the note.

The perfect goddamn gentleman, he thought grimly.

Grant turned away and stuffed his feet into flip-flops. Then he headed out the door, making a beeline for the beach. He had his cell phone in a pouch strapped to his arm in case she woke up and needed anything.

Right now, he needed space.

He kicked the shoes off under a log and took off running along the shore, breathing evenly as the ocean air filled his lungs. He moved to the edge of the water where the sand was packed firmly with seawater. A pair of doves flitted across the sand in front of him, looking for specks of food. They scattered as Grant ran through, then reassembled a few feet up the beach.

Grant kept running, the scent of Anna still clinging to his skin. Christ, he probably should have showered or something. He could still smell her everywhere, still feel the softness of her touch on his skin. He tried closing his eyes, but all that did was make him dizzy as he conjured the image of her coppery hair spread across the pillow, those green eyes going wide with an emotion he couldn't name.

He couldn't name it, but he knew it. He'd felt it too, goddammit.

Stop this now, he commanded himself, not sure if he meant the thoughts or this thing with Anna. Probably both.

Grant kicked up his pace to a punishing speed, running out onto the loose sand until his lungs and his calves were screaming. By the time he'd finished his run, he was breathing hard and drenched in sweat.

He doubled over, anchoring his palms on his knees, fighting to catch his breath as he dripped sweat into the sand. He should have at least brought a shirt so he had something to mop his face with. He could cool off with a dip in the ocean, or maybe he could run back to his place and take a cool shower with Anna pressed against him, slick and soapy and laughing as she twirled under the spray.

No. No swimming. No cool showers with beautiful women. *You don't deserve any of that.*

Grant winced as his phone vibrated on his arm.

Anna, he thought, fumbling it out of the pouch.

"Mac" the readout said, and Grant tried not to feel disappointed.

"Hey," he said , his breathing still labored from the run. "What's up?"

"Please tell me you're not answering the phone in the middle of something sweaty and illicit."

"Sweaty, yes. Illicit, no. Not that it's any of your business."

"I hope you didn't leave your houseguest alone and in need of medical attention."

"She's asleep," Grant muttered, not bothering to ask how Mac knew Anna had stayed the night. Somehow, Mac knew everything.

Maybe not everything.

"So is there a reason you're calling so early?" Grant asked, trying to keep his tone upbeat. "I mean besides harassing me about Anna?"

"I seem to recall you harassing me in a similar fashion only a few months ago. Married life is good; you should try it sometime."

"I'll leave that to the rest of the Patton siblings."

"That's actually why I'm calling. Mom issued an order last night."

"Someone gave her missile launch codes again?"

"Not missiles. Worse. She wants all of her children present at Sheridan's wedding. You know what that means."

Grant resisted the urge to groan. He closed his eyes and concentrated on not balling his fists at his sides. "Why do you need me? You've been able to burrow your way into everything from military personnel files to police records for every man Sheri ever dated."

"And yet, our brother's location eludes me. You're the only one who knows where he is, Grant."

"We haven't spoken for a long time."

"And you're the only one who knows *why* that is. It's none of my business."

"Like that's ever stopped you from meddling before."

"Please reach out to him, Grant. It would mean a lot to Sheri. And to Mom."

Grant closed his eyes again, listening to the sound of the waves crashing on the shore behind him. He took a deep breath and nodded, even though he knew Mac couldn't see him. Or hell, maybe he could. Mac seemed to know everything.

Not this.

"Fine. I'll do what I can."

"That's all we can ask. Now get back and attend to your guest."

"Who put you in charge of the universe?"

"I did," Mac said and hung up.

Grant grunted at the dead air, then drew the phone from his ear and stared at it a few beats. Then he pulled up the keypad for dialing.

Schwartz's number wasn't in his contacts list. Mac was too smart for that, and Grant was much too careful. The only place it existed was in the recesses of his brain.

He sighed and punched in the first few digits. He closed his eyes, hesitating. Then he punched in the rest of the numbers. Pressing the phone against his ear, he listened to the hollow sound of the ring. It trilled once, then twice. Grant's hands were shaking, and his throat felt too tight.

The call clicked over to voicemail.

"It's me. You know what to do."

Then a beep, followed by silence.

"Hey," Grant said, annoyed at the waver in his voice. "It's

me. Grant." He shook his head, not sure if he was lame for identifying himself, or presumptuous for thinking he might not have to. "Look, Sheri's getting married in a few days. You'd really like the guy she's marrying, Sam? The whole family would really love it if you could make it. I know you don't get out much, but—"

He stopped himself, realizing how idiotic he sounded. What did he really know, anyway?

"So it would be really great if you'd come. She's still living on Kauai, and the service is at Kauai Christian Fellowship at three o'clock on Saturday the twenty-ninth. Call me if you want details, okay?"

He hesitated, ready to switch off the call. Then he cleared his throat. "I miss you."

His hands felt cold as he disconnected the call. He stuffed the phone back into his armband and ran hard all the way home. As he unlocked the door, he felt himself pasting a Boy Scout smile into place. The woodsy, grassy smell of the body wash he kept in his shower hung in the air, and Grant pictured Anna standing towel-dried and barefoot in the kitchen, naked beneath one of his dress shirts.

You don't own any dress shirts, idiot.

Probably needed to remedy that before Sheri's wedding.

"Anna?" he called, heart pounding as he rounded the corner to the kitchen. That's when he realized there was no scent of coffee in the air. His coffee cup was right where he'd left it, untouched.

Wait, it had definitely been touched. He peered at the note. A scrawl of loopy, girlie handwriting filled the space beneath his words. He picked up the note and read.

Grant, Thank you for the kind gesture, but I'm afraid I'm not much of a coffee drinker. I know I can lose my Portland residency for that, but I'm more of a hot tea kind of girl. I'm heading out to find some, then off to an early meeting with your mom and sister. Let's catch up later to talk about the paintball wedding.

There was a string of *xoxoxoxo* and Grant tried to remember which one was the sign for hugs and which one for kisses.

It doesn't matter, idiot. You don't deserve any of them.

He crumpled the note and trudged down the hall to wash the scent of her off his skin.

• • •

Anna glanced at her watch, relieved to see she was ten minutes early. Janelle plunked down in the seat beside her, her coffee cup clattering in its saucer as she stirred in a giant spoonful of sugar.

"They're not here yet, so dish," Janelle whispered. "Did you sleep with him? How was he? Did you come?"

"Shh!" Anna looked around the coffee shop, grateful no one had turned to stare. She looked back at her sister and shook her head. "His mom and his sister will be here any minute. You really think this is the right time to discuss Grant's prowess in the sack?"

"Good point," Janelle said, blowing on her coffee. "We should wait till they get here. They'll probably want details, too."

Anna flipped open her wedding notebook and glared at her sister. "What makes you so sure I slept with him? Maybe he just played nursemaid to me all night and made sure I didn't have any reactions to the centipede bite."

"Please. I saw the way that man looked at you all day. Like you were a gooey Danish and he'd been starving for a week."

"Thank you for that image." Still, Anna couldn't help but smile a little at the thought.

"So tell me all about it," Janelle said. "He looks like he'd be amazing in the sack."

Anna tried to look stern, but the corners of her mouth turned up completely against her will. Janelle squealed and elbowed her in the ribs.

"I knew it! He's totally hot. And definitely not the type to try to railroad you into marriage and babies and all that other shit you don't want."

"Right," Anna said, digging out her clicky pen and two notebooks packed with information about Sheridan Patton's wedding plans. "He's definitely not that type."

She kept her eyes on the notebook, ignoring the funny feeling in her gut as she picked up her Earl Grey and took a sip. Janelle stirred some more creamer into her coffee and sighed.

"Good for you knowing exactly what you want and going after it. Or what you *don't* want, I guess I should say. Just give me a little dirt, Anna-Banana—was he rough and dirty, or sweet and gentle?"

Anna bit her lip and tried not to smile.

"Both?" Janelle clapped her hands together with glee. "I knew it. He's perfect in bed, too?"

"Shh!" Anna glanced to the left, then to the right, hoping like hell no one could hear them. "His mom and sister will be here any minute."

"What? Every mother wants to know she raised her son to be a considerate lover who's attentive to his partner's orgasm."

"Who's attentive to his partner's orgasm?"

Anna closed her eyes and willed the ground to swallow her up. Beside her, Janelle whispered, "Oops," and slunk down in her chair.

Opening her eyes, Anna stood up and turned to greet Grant's sister, mother, and the maid of honor. It was the latter who stood beaming at Anna, waiting for a response to the question.

"Kelli," Anna said, giving her old friend a hug and a subtle death glare before turning to greet the bride and her mother. "Can I get you ladies anything? Coffee? Tea?"

"The skinny on who you slept with," Kelli said, plunking down in a chair beside Anna and grinning. "You're sitting down to breakfast with a newlywed and a soon-to-be newlywed, which means we're pretty much sex obsessed. Come on, dish a little so we can hear about someone's sex life besides our own."

Sheri rolled her eyes at her best friend's brazenness as she gave Anna a warm hug. Anna glanced at the mother of the bride, who looked surprisingly unruffled by the discussion. Catching Anna's look of alarm, Stella waved a hand in the air.

"Please, dear. With Kelli as my daughter-in-law, you don't honestly think I'm offended by a little frank discussion of human sexuality? Besides, I raised all my sons and daughter to be comfortable with the subject and the way their bodies function."

"She used G.I. Joe and my Wonder Woman action figure to act out scenes from *How Babies are Made*," Sheri said helpfully, signaling the waitress for a cup of coffee as she sat down beside Kelli. "Wonder Woman held on to her battle-ax the whole time, and G.I. Joe had an AK-47 strapped to his back."

"This explains a lot about Patton sexuality," Kelli said, grabbing a sugar packet from the middle of the table as the waitress began pouring coffee all around. Anna placed a hand over her teacup so she wouldn't be added to the lineup of coffee refills. "I have finally gotten Mac to remove the ankle holster before coming to bed, so that's progress," Kelli continued. "Of course he almost lost a toe the other day when the knife he'd stashed behind our headboard came crashing down as he tossed me on the bed. Note to all women bedding Patton men: frisk them well before you take your clothes off."

Anna swallowed and struggled to come up with a good way to change the subject. She clicked her pen at a frantic pace, her other palm sweating as she pressed it against the cover of her notebook. Beside her, Janelle made a feeble effort to divert the conversation.

"The weather sure is nice today. Do you think—"

"There is a certain glow about you this morning, Anna," Stella said, eyeing her up and down over the rim of her coffee cup. "Either you're coming down with something, or merely coming. Which is it, dear?"

"Mom!" Sheri rolled her eyes and shot Anna a sympathetic look. "You've been spending too much time with Kelli. Can we please not badger my wedding planner about her sex life?"

"Very well, dear," Stella said, glancing at Anna once more. She sipped her coffee again and offered a coy smile. "But don't think for a moment I didn't notice the fragrance of my son's favorite body wash emanating from your person. Now, is everything all squared away with the floral arrangements?"

Anna opened her mouth to reply, her cheeks flaming as she flipped through the notebook to find the right page. Beside her, Kelli was practically bouncing in her seat.

"Whoa, whoa, whoa!" she called, making a T with one hand perpendicular atop the other. "Time out here. Anna, you're sleeping with Grant?"

Janelle grinned and bounced right along with Kelli. "If this is all out in the open now, do we at least get to know details?"

"Oh, for the love of God." Anna dropped her pen on the table and covered her face with her hands. "Please say we're not really having this conversation in front of my client, her maid of honor, and the mother of the bride who won a military medal for marksmanship."

"Three medals, dear," Stella said. "But that's beside the point. I can't say I'm terribly surprised. Grant did seem awfully taken with you when I spoke with him on the phone a few days ago."

"He mentioned me?" Anna pried her hands away from her face and blinked at Stella, her urge to know details overpowering her urge to crawl under the table. "What did he say?"

"Just that he was quite looking forward to doing some photography work with Sheridan's wedding planner, and that he enjoyed your company over dinner the other night.

Obviously, I wasn't aware of the extent to which he enjoyed it, but it all makes sense now."

Anna swallowed, studying Stella's face for any sign of judgment or anger. There was none, which didn't necessarily mean anything. The Patton family was notoriously difficult to read.

"He's a truly talented photographer," Anna said, picking up her pen again. "The images he captured yesterday are breathtaking."

"Sounds like that's not the only thing Grant's got that's taking your breath away," Kelli said, grinning. "Seriously, those hands. Stella, did you take some sort of performance-enhancing drugs during pregnancy to ensure your sons all had hands the size of catcher's mitts?"

Janelle giggled. "You know what they say about men with big hands."

"And I can assure you it's true," Kelli said, lifting her coffee mug in a mock toast while Stella regarded her new daughter-in-law like some sort of colorful exotic bird.

Stella took another sip of coffee, then turned back to Anna. "So when you saw him this morning, did he happen to mention if he reached Schwartz?"

"Schwartz?" Anna shook her head, not sure whether to press for information or to feel guilty for intruding on Grant's personal life more than she already had. It wasn't every day she followed up a passionate romp by having breakfast with the man's entire tribe of female relations. "We, uh, didn't cross paths this morning. He got up early to run, and I had to leave before he got back so we could make it to this meeting." Anna swallowed and pushed her notebook across the table. "So if you'll look here at page thirty-six, these are the flowers we'll be—"

"Grant's asking Schwartz to come?" Sheri flashed a hopeful smile at her mother. "Wow, it's been years. I'm not even sure I'd recognize him."

"I wouldn't get my hopes up, dear," Stella said, patting her daughter's hand. "Still, if anyone can talk him into it, it's Grant."

Anna felt an odd swell of pride that made zero sense. Grant wasn't hers, and she had no idea what they'd been talking about. Still, she couldn't resist the urge to pry just a little. "Grant and Schwartz are close?"

"They were inseparable as kids," Sheri said, looking a little wistful. "Not as much after Schwartz's accident."

"Accident?"

"His Humvee hit an IED in Iraq," Stella said, looking down at her hands. "Schwartz's entire unit was killed, and he was badly injured. Still walks with a bit of a limp when he's anyplace humid, but other than that, he ultimately recovered—physically, anyway."

"Emotionally, he's the human equivalent of an iceberg," Sheri added. "He's basically a hermit. None of us even knows where he's living right now."

"Except for Grant," Anna added, and Stella nodded.

"But even that connection is shaky at best." Her usual stoic expression had been replaced by something more maternal, more haunted. Anna ached to reach across the table and squeeze her hand, but she held back.

Sheri pulled the notebook in front of her and pressed her palm against a page containing photos of colorful floral arrangements. "It would be great if Schwartz made it to the wedding, but I won't hold my breath."

"At least you know he'll send a gift," Kelli offered. "I've never even met the guy and he sent flowers for my birthday last month, plus he found out where we were honeymooning in Greece and had a gift certificate waiting in our hotel room so we could take a romantic sunset cruise."

"All my kids are thoughtful," Stella said proudly. "And excellent shots."

"Huh," Anna said, trying to imagine this mysterious, reclusive brother and connect the dots between Grant's cheerful Boy Scout demeanor. It made no sense. Then again, control-freak Mac didn't seem to have much in common with either brother.

Still, something told her there was more to this story. And maybe it was connected to Grant's incessant need to be perfect.

"Well, Stella," Anna said brightly. "You've certainly bred a diverse batch of offspring."

"You don't know the half of it, dear." Stella smiled and signaled the waitress for more coffee. "And they're proving to have entertaining choices in mates."

Her gaze held Anna's for a few beats longer than comfortable. Anna swallowed and looked away, flipping open a blank notebook and scribbling a single word in the margin.

Desiderium she wrote, reminding herself to google the title Grant had given to that file full of photos.

She took a deep breath and clicked her pen again.

Chapter Eleven

Grant watched Anna as she handed an envelope to the caterer and said farewell. She was covered from head to toe with splotches of red and blue paint, and her hair stuck to the sides of her flushed cheeks.

He'd never seen a more beautiful woman in his whole life.

He fired off a final shot and stuffed his camera back in its bag. Zipping it up, he strode over to her and smiled. "You look like you could use a shower."

She grinned and looked down at herself. "I wasn't planning to get involved in the paintball portion of the ceremony, but it looked like too much fun."

"Can't say I blame you. I almost wish you hadn't instituted a don't-shoot-the -photographer rule."

"It's a rule I insist on at all my weddings," she said. "Along with 'don't pet the badgers' and 'don't startle the sword swallower.'"

"Good rules to have," Grant said, thinking how much he'd like to pull her into the shower and press her up against the wall, cupping her soapy breasts from behind as he drove into her and—

"Have you ever done that before?" she asked.

"What?" Grant swallowed, wondering for a moment if she'd read his thoughts.

"That," she said, pointing out across the river beyond the wedding site. A pair of standup paddleboarders glided slowly across the water, their paddles making ripples on the surface of the Wailua. "I've always wanted to try that," she said. "It looks like so much fun."

"It just so happens I have two boards at home."

"Two?"

He shrugged. "I bought an extra so my brother can join me when he visits."

"Schwartz?"

The word hit him like a punch in his gut, and it took him a couple beats to catch his breath. "No, Mac. Schwartz doesn't visit."

Her cheeks pinkened a little at that, and she glanced away. "Sorry, of course. Your mom and sister were talking the other morning about Schwartz. Is he coming to the wedding?"

Grant swallowed and shook his head. "I don't know. I don't think so. My mom asked me to invite him, but—" Grant cleared his throat again. "Come on. You can shower at my place while I grab the boards out of storage. I'll have you paddling like a pro in no time."

"Really?"

"Sure. You're done here, right?"

"Pretty much. Janelle volunteered for cleanup duty again, so I just need to pay the DJ and say good-bye to the bride and groom."

"Go do that and I'll pull the car around."

Anna grinned and looked down at herself. "I don't think you want me on your upholstery with all this paint on my clothes."

"Good point. You should take them off."

She rolled her eyes. "Nice try."

"Okay, fine. I have a tarp in back we can use to cover the seats."

"You take the Boy Scout motto pretty seriously," she said, stepping away from him as she waved to the bride. "Be prepared."

"Not always," Grant murmured, watching her walk away from him as he considered how very unprepared he was to have Anna in his life. How unworthy of having someone willing to trust him with her darkest secret when he couldn't do the same for her.

Once she'd bid farewell to the wedding party and climbed into the car, Grant drove back to his place. Back at the house, he fought the urge to join her in the shower and fulfill his soapy fantasies. He wanted nothing more than to slide into the shower beside her, to let his hands slick over her breasts and hips and ass.

But something told him to keep his distance. He'd seen the look in her eye, and he'd felt the stirring of something sharp and terrifying in himself.

Keep your distance. Don't fall for her, dumbass.

So Grant busied himself getting the paddleboards out of storage while Anna stripped off her paint-stained clothes and climbed naked and beautiful into the shower. Or at least that's what Grant imagined. He imagined it so thoroughly that he was half-hard by the time she emerged from the bathroom.

He was fully hard the instant he saw her in a bikini.

"Jesus."

Anna laughed and did a small pirouette. "You like it? I wasn't sure red was my color, but I got it on sale before the trip. It's a little skimpier than I'd normally wear, but Janelle insisted."

"God bless your sister."

She grinned and closed the distance between them. His hand went around her automatically, pressing into the small of her back where a small tattoo of a goldfish swam across her spine. She stood on tiptoe to kiss him, and Grant kissed her back, hating how traitorously his body craved her, even while his brain was screaming at him to keep his distance.

Thankfully, Anna was first to draw back.

"Sorry, I don't mean to get all relationshipy on you. I appreciated how we kept things professional at the wedding. I just wanted a kiss."

"Not a problem," Grant said, wondering if he should kiss her again or run like hell.

"Come on. I'm excited to learn to standup paddle. Are we going out on the ocean right out here?"

"No, it's too rough here. Hanalei Bay is perfect, especially this time of day. I've already got the boards on the roof rack, and it's only a twenty-minute drive."

"Excellent!" she called, and skipped off ahead of him, her flip-flops smacking the ground while his heart did the same against his rib cage.

They talked easily all the way to Hanalei, with Grant pointing out landmarks and favorite restaurants and Anna chattering about his sister's wedding. "It's coming together nicely," she said, brushing her red-gold hair behind her ears. "I think your mom felt a little ripped off when Mac and Kelli decided to go for a spur-of-the-moment, family-only kinda wedding, so she's making sure Sheri's wedding is a grander affair. Your sister's been great to work with, by the way. Super down-to-earth and not the least bit bridezilla."

"My sister's pretty easygoing," Grant said. "She probably had to be, growing up with so many brothers."

"Who was she closest to?" Anna asked.

Grant felt tension prickle his arms as he scouted for a parking spot. "I was the youngest by eleven months, so she mostly saw me as the baby. Well, at least until high school when I grew a foot taller and started bench-pressing her as a stunt at family barbecues. And Mac—well, he was a lot older than the rest of us. He left home right away and spent a lot of time overseas with military operations. You know Mac— he's not exactly the warm and cuddly teddy-bear type."

"Like you?" she asked, grinning at him. "That's exactly the phrase Kelli used to describe you before we ever met— the big-teddy-bear brother."

Grant smiled, keeping his eyes on the road. "I'm not sure whether to be flattered or take it as an insult to my masculinity."

"No insult intended. Teddy bears are sexy."

"I'll try not to think about that the next time I buy one for my nephews."

Anna laughed as Grant angled into a parking spot. "So Schwartz? That's who Sheri was closest to?"

Grant swallowed and pulled the parking break. "I guess so. When we were younger, anyway. Probably not as close as he and I were, but pretty close. I imagine it was tough for her being the only girl."

She studied him, and Grant focused on not blinking, not showing any signs of discomfort. When she nodded, he felt a twinge of relief. "Just trying to get a read on the family dynamic here."

"Good luck with that," he said, and pushed open his door.

He began unhooking the boards from the top of the car, while Anna busied herself grabbing the paddles he pointed out in the back of the rig. By the time they were out on the water's edge, Grant was feeling hot and sweaty.

He was pretty sure it was the sun and not the sight of Anna moving around in that red bikini.

They carried the boards out into the water, and Grant showed her how to lay the paddle perpendicular across the front.

"Okay, you want to start out on your knees," Grant said, demonstrating the position as he used one hand to hold her board steady.

"I find starting out on my knees usually helps speed things along," she said, giving him a salacious grin. "Sorry, I've been spending too much time around Kelli."

"Or too much time on your knees." He grinned back. "Never mind, no such thing. Okay, brace the paddle across the front of the board like this. You can use that as a support system to get yourself standing upright, or you can stay down on your knees for a while to get used to the feel of being on the board."

"No, I want to try standing," she said, scrunching her

face into a look of intense concentration as she followed his directions and got to her feet. She wobbled a little at first, then stood strong, her knees bent a little as she got her balance. "Hey, this isn't as hard as it looks."

"It's harder in a bay like this than it is on a river or a lake," he said, admiring her form. Well, admiring her body, too, but also her form. "You've got great balance."

"Thanks. Fifteen years of yoga. Remind me sometime to show you how I can put my ankles behind my head."

She gave him another grin, and Grant tried to decide if she was kidding or not. Probably not, he decided, watching the limber way she maneuvered on the board, starting to paddle before he even had a chance to show her how.

"You're a natural," he said, dipping his own paddle into the water to keep up with her. "Change your grip up like this and you'll have more control."

"Like this?"

"Perfect. And you want the blade of the paddle facing the other way. An easy way to remember is to always have the logo facing forward. It'll give you more power on your stroke."

"Got it," she said, and mimicked his movements exactly. "Hey, this is fun."

They paddled in silence for a bit, with Anna testing out different strokes and wobbling only a little when a small wave caught her board. Grant gave her a few more pointers and then dropped back, letting her get the hang of things on her own. She had a real knack for the sport.

He kept himself a few strokes behind her, admiring the curve of her backside and the scattering of tattoos on her body. He'd been too preoccupied to study them when he'd had her naked in his bed the other day. There was the feather on her ankle, a sunflower on her shoulder blade, the goldfish in the small of her back, and some more ink on the left side of her rib cage that must have hurt like hell.

"What's the significance of the starfish?" he called, gesturing to her ribs as he angled his board past her.

"There's this story about a guy walking down the beach and seeing a kid standing on the shore surrounded by all these starfish that have washed up on the beach," she began, driving her paddle into the water to turn. "The guy walks up and says, 'What are you doing?' and the kid says, 'I'm throwing starfish back in the water so they don't die.' The guy looks at him like he's fucking crazy, right? 'There are thousands of starfish here, and they're drying out and dying in the sun as we speak. You can't possibly make a difference.'" Anna drove her paddle into the water again, turning so she faced him. "The kid looks at him, picks up another starfish, and chucks it into the ocean. 'Made a difference to that one.'"

Grant felt a prickle of emotion snake its way up his arms, and her gaze held his as she smiled. "I always liked that story," she said. "I got the tattoo as a reminder never to lose sight of the small ways I can make a difference in people's lives, whether I'm doing my job or going about my day-to-day life."

"Wow," Grant said, finding his words at last. "And you call me a Boy Scout. That's pretty admirable. Great artwork, too."

"Thanks!" she said, grinning as she switched sides with her paddle, driving the blade into the water to keep herself headed straight. "It's my favorite of the four. Do you just have the one on your arm?"

"Yeah. Got it during basic training. It's the Marine Corps emblem, along with some other custom details. I got it after my first tour."

"Yeah?"

She seemed to be waiting for him to share more, but Grant didn't want to go there. He'd rather hear about her.

He drove his paddle into the water, catching up to her easily. "I have to admit, I haven't dated a lot of women with ink."

She grinned and looked at him. "Are we dating? I thought we were just fucking."

Grant lost his balance. He started to catch himself, swaying like a drunk guy in a bouncy house, but the wind caught him just right and down he went.

Splash!

The ankle leash on his board kept it from getting away, and the water only came up to his shoulders, but still. He came up sputtering to find Anna laughing so hard she was doubled at the waist.

"Sorry, I don't mean to laugh."

"Yes you do," Grant said, spitting out a mouthful of saltwater as he grinned at her.

"You're so easily shocked, I can't help it."

"I'm not normally," he said, ducking under his board and resurfacing beside hers. "It's the bluntness that gets me. You can fire a rocket launcher ten feet away and I swear I won't flinch."

"I'll try to remember to pick up a rocket launcher the next time I'm at Walmart."

Grant grinned and looked up at her legs. God, she was

beautiful. He remembered the feel of those legs wrapped around his back and he wanted her all over again. Badly.

"For the record," he said. "We're not just fucking."

"No?"

"No. I don't know what we're doing, exactly, but it's more than that. We also have an excellent professional relationship."

"Can't argue with that," she said, dipping her paddle in the water to hold the board steady. "Are you going to demonstrate how to get back up on your board?"

"Nope." He reached up and caught her ankle. "I'm going to teach you how to fall."

She shrieked with surprise as Grant tugged her leg. She toppled toward him, and Grant caught her easily with one arm, relishing the warmth of her body and the smell of her shampoo as she splashed, laughing against his chest.

"Jerk!" she yelled, her laughter contradicting any genuine annoyance.

"Sorry," he said, not the least bit sorry. She felt damn good wet and wriggling in his arms. He let go of her with one arm and grabbed her paddle, setting it on top of his board beside his own so it wouldn't get away. Her board was still tethered to her ankle, just like his was, so they weren't going anywhere.

He wrapped his arms around her again, pretty sure he'd never felt anything so deliciously perfect in his life. They bobbed together like that for a moment, the ocean water making a soothing cocoon around their bodies. The sun was warm on his back, and he filled his lungs with the heady scent of ocean air and something coconuty in Anna's sunscreen. A pack of surfers chased waves off in the distance, and only one lone fisherman had nabbed a spot on the pier.

He'd never seen the place this quiet.

"This is nice," she said, looking up at him. "The water feels so good. So warm."

"Mmmhmm," Grant replied. He should probably let her go. He'd do it in just a minute. The way she moved against him was making all the blood leave his brain to occupy another part of his body that was probably becoming damn obvious to her by now.

As though reading his thoughts, Anna grinned and wrapped her legs around his waist. She pressed her lower body against him, hands on his shoulders, as her eyes flashed with something that drained the last teaspoon of blood from his brain.

"Is that a tube of sunscreen in your pocket, or are you happy to see me?"

"If I weren't a gentleman, I'd suggest you squeeze it and find out."

She laughed, throwing her head back in a way that made him want to devour her shoulders and neck and throat and collarbones. He moved his hands to her butt, holding her against his growing arousal. He glanced behind her toward the pier. It was thirty feet away, so even if someone strolled out there, they probably couldn't see beneath the water. Still.

"Grant?"

"Hmm?"

"This bikini's pretty tiny."

"Thank God," he murmured, pressing himself against her.

"But it might surprise you to know it has a pocket."

The randomness of her words surprised him enough that he tore his eyes off the pier. He blinked at her, the paddleboard bumping against his elbow. "What?"

"A pocket. In the back of my bikini bottoms. It's probably supposed to hold a car key or something, but you know what else it can hold?"

The grin had spread wide across her face, and Grant's balls ached at the thought of her spreading anything else for him. He slid his hand to the spot just below the small of her back and felt the crinkle of cellophane.

"You didn't seriously bring a condom out here."

"I'm learning from your Boy Scout ways," she said, her breath warm on his neck now. She nibbled his earlobe as she ground hard against his erection. "Be prepared, right?"

He didn't answer her. Not with words, anyway. As his mouth found hers, he slid one hand from her ass to the front of her bikini bottoms. He slipped one finger inside, groaning when he found her slippery and wet from more than just seawater.

"Christ," he murmured, kissing her harder.

"I want you," she whispered. "Grab the condom."

She drew back so their upper bodies were angled apart, even as their lower bodies pressed tight together. She held herself away from him, grinning, with her fingers laced behind his neck. "As far as anyone knows on the beach, we're just a couple embracing in the water. Maybe kissing a little."

Her words were a faint buzz in his ears, and though he knew it was crazy, he found himself fumbling the condom out of her bikini pocket. He tore off the wrapper, shoving it in the Velcro pocket of his swim trunks so it wouldn't float away.

"So conscientious," she murmured, kissing his neck. "Such a responsible, upstanding citizen."

"Who's about to do something highly illegal," Grant murmured, not caring all that much.

She drew back again, fingers laced behind his neck as Grant slid the condom on as discreetly as possible. Was this even safe in saltwater? He wasn't sure, but part of him didn't care.

"I googled it, in case you're wondering. As long as you maintain an erection the whole time so the condom doesn't slip off, we should be safe."

"Leave it to you," he murmured, not sure if he meant the preemptive research or her frankness about the whole thing.

"Are you complaining?"

"God, no. Though I sure as hell hope those people on the beach don't complain to the police."

"Relax," she said, leaning away from him again as she ground her pelvis against him beneath the water. "For all anyone knows, we're out here discussing politics."

"Or baseball."

"Or existential theories of existence preceding essence."

"Or beer."

"Kiss me."

He obeyed, taking her mouth with bruising force so he wouldn't give in to the temptation to cup her breasts in his hands. That would be too visible to anyone on shore, but what was happening beneath the surface—

"God, you're hard," she murmured, pulling back to smile at him. She released his neck, letting her upper body fall back to float on the surface of the water, while her legs wrapped tight around him, anchoring them together.

Grant groaned and slid his hand between their bodies. He pushed her bikini bottoms to one side, expecting to go slow, to take his time.

But Anna had other ideas.

She straightened up and anchored her hands on his shoulders, pressing her body down to take him all in one slick stroke.

Grant closed his eyes and cursed under his breath. He felt her fingers twine around his neck again, and she rose up in the water, then sheathed him completely.

"Jesus, Grant," she gasped, grinding against him, moving her hips. Her eyes were wide with something that looked a lot like wonder as she sank down on him again. "The water—holy Christ, this feels good."

He grinned and slid his hands into the small of her back, amazed at the weightlessness of her, at the slippery heat between her legs. The paddleboards bobbed along the surface on either side of them, creating an odd sort of privacy shield. He felt one of the tethers winding around his arm, but couldn't stop to free himself.

"You feel fucking amazing," he groaned as she rode him with aching slowness. Above the water, their bodies barely moved. Below the surface, it was another world entirely. She was hot and tight around him, her body gripping him as she ground herself against his abdomen.

He was going to last about ten seconds at this rate, so he said a prayer of thanks when she gasped in his ear.

"Oh, God!"

Grant replied by gripping her hips tighter, pressing her down onto him, driving himself deeper, matching her thrust for thrust.

"Yes," she hissed, closing her eyes and biting down on his shoulder. Grant winced, but kept going, feeling his body start to give as she clenched and spasmed around him. He was three beats behind her, so close.

"Holy mother-of—"

She smothered his words with a kiss, while the orgasm rocketed him to another planet, sending pulse after pulse of pleasure though his cock, his hips, his arms, his legs, through every molecule of his body.

When she pulled back, she was smiling at him. She planted a kiss on his forehead, then his nose, before drawing back to look him in the eye. "I've had that on my bucket list forever. Thank you."

"My pleasure," he said, too shell-shocked to give much thought to whether that had meant something to her or if he'd just been her ticket to fulfilling a kinky fantasy. Did it matter?

She slid away from him, adjusting her bikini bottoms and untangling the paddleboard tether that had managed to wind its way around her leg.

Grant concentrated on shoving the condom into his pocket, saying a silent apology to the marine life. He glanced at the pier, then back at the beach. A grizzled-looking fisherman was bent over his hook, finessing his bait into place. Back on shore, a middle-aged woman dug through a bright red cooler, while a twentysomething couple strolled hand in hand along the water, their eyes cast downward in search of seashells.

No one seemed to have noticed anything.

"That was incredible," she said, and Grant turned his attention back to her.

"It was."

"I don't suppose you have any water back in your car?"

"Ocean's not enough for you?"

She grinned and slugged him. "To drink, dork. I thought I saw a cooler in back?"

"Yeah, come on. Let's replenish our reserves before we do any more paddling."

He showed her how to climb back on the board, staying on his knees to cover the short distance to the beach. When they reached the shore, he grabbed one board under each arm as Anna grabbed both paddles.

"If you want to wait here with the boards, I'll grab the water."

"Might want to empty your pockets, too," she said, grinning as she sank down into the sand, stretching those glorious legs out in front of her.

Grant shook his head and turned away. He jogged back toward the parking area wondering how the hell it was possible he could want her again.

You know how.

He'd almost reached the car when a woman stepped out of the shade of a palm tree with her hand extended. "Afternoon, sir. I'm Sarah Marshfield from KITV news. We're filming a piece on the history of the Hanalei pier, and got the loveliest shot of you and your wife embracing out there. Can I ask you a few questions for the broadcast?"

• • •

Anna laughed all the way to Kapaa.

"So there's going to be footage of us screwing on the news?" She sat grinning in the passenger seat, her bikini still damp with seawater and flecked with sand. He loved that she hadn't bothered to cover up with a pair of shorts or a T-shirt like most women did. Her hair was loose around her shoulders and speckled with salt crystals.

Grant shook his head, pleased she found the whole TV thing amusing instead of mortifying. "They thought we were just kissing," he said. "I couldn't exactly tell them they'd just filmed porn."

"That makes the whole thing even better. I wonder if I could get a copy of it after it airs?"

"There's something to add to your family's video library."

She nodded and looked out the window, the smile still lighting up her face. Grant turned his eyes back to the road, feeling warm and satiated in a way that didn't just come from an afternoon of exercise and sunshine.

"This is what I love about you," he blurted, a little surprised by his own words.

He watched her head swivel back toward him, something odd in her expression. "Love?"

"No. I mean—you know what I mean."

She nodded, looking uncertain. "Sure. I think so."

Grant put his gaze back on the road, trying to make the words come out right. "I just mean it's great that you're not freaked out by something like that. Most women I know would be embarrassed or weirded out or angry. Hell, most women I know would never have sex in a public place like that. I love that you're so—"

"Different." Her voice had gone flat, and Grant looked over to see she wasn't smiling anymore.

"That's a good thing," he clarified, not sure where she'd taken offense. "A great thing, really. I love that you're not like most women."

She fell quiet again, her eyes cast out the passenger window toward the road. Grant gripped the steering wheel, not sure if he should apologize or wait it out to see if she had something to say.

He'd just pulled into the driveway of his house when she turned to face him again.

"There's something I need to tell you, Grant."

"Another confession?"

She nodded. "A bigger one this time."

He pulled the parking brake and killed the engine. Something in her voice made his gut cinch up tighter than a ball of rubber bands, and he tried to keep the dread from showing on his face.

"Okay. Let's hear it."

Anna licked her lips, and he watched her chest rise and fall as she took a steadying breath. "I lied to you."

Chapter Twelve

The moment the words were out of her mouth, Anna knew she couldn't take them back.

So she said them again. "I lied."

Something dark flashed over Grant's face. "This isn't about condoms and saltwater, is it?"

"Definitely not." She managed a halfhearted smile, but shook her head. What she needed to say was too important to let herself get derailed by sex. "Can we go inside? I'd rather have this conversation in a house than a car."

"You're scaring me," he said, and the vulnerability in his voice made Anna want to cradle him in her arms and forget this whole damn thing. She was wavering when Grant pushed his door open.

"Come on. I'll grab us a cold drink and we can sit on the couch and talk."

She let him lead her inside, but she didn't sit down on the couch. She was wet and sandy, and she shivered a little in the air-conditioning. Grant moved to the kitchen where he busied himself pulling two glasses from the cupboard. Anna moved past him, opening the door to the lanai. She walked out into the sunshine, hesitating at the edge of the chair. It was where she'd been sitting the first time they'd kissed. Before she'd opened her legs and her heart and her mind and told him everything—

Not everything.

"Here," he said behind her, and she spun around to see him standing there with a glass of ice water. She took it from him, her hands shaking, as Grant folded himself into the same chair where he'd been seated a little over a week ago.

Had it only been that long?

He set his water on the table and turned to face her. "Okay, so what's on your mind?"

Anna took a drink of water, then a steadying breath. She set her glass on the table and began to pace.

"I lied to you," she repeated, not meeting his eyes.

"You mentioned that. Can we get to the specifics?"

"Right. See, the thing is, I want to get married."

"Right now?"

She turned at the alarm in his voice and saw the color had drained from his face.

"No—I mean, not to you. Or maybe to you, I don't know. I'm not proposing, Grant, and I'm not trying to say I want to date exclusively or settle down or move in together or start looking for rings or—"

"What *are* you saying?"

She stopped pacing and turned to look at him. To *really* look at him. His face was still pale, and his hands were clenched so tightly in his lap he looked like he might rip his fingers out of their sockets.

"I'm saying I've tried very hard for a number of years to convince myself that marriage wasn't my thing. That it was okay for other people, but not something I ever planned to do myself." She pressed her lips together, trying to find the right words. "The thing is, I don't think it was ever that I didn't *want* it. It was more that I thought I didn't *deserve* it."

He was staring at her stone-faced, an expression that left Anna feeling like an elephant was sitting on her chest. She turned away and began pacing again, determined to say what she needed to say before she broke down like a big idiot.

"I haven't trusted my own instincts for a long time. Between missing all the signs that my sister's husband was a jerk, and my own stupid near miss with a guy who turned out to have a wife already, I had every reason to think I couldn't rely on my own judgment. That I couldn't trust myself."

"Okay," he said, his voice low and guarded.

"I spent my childhood blaming myself for my parents' divorce and a lot of my adulthood blaming myself for my sister's divorce."

"Right," he said slowly, and she saw him nod in her peripheral vision. "And we talked about how that's a shitty thing to do. None of that was your fault, Anna. You can't blame yourself."

"You're right," she said, turning to face him again. She stood with her hands limp at her sides, the relief at being understood mixing in the pit of her stomach with the dread of what she was saying. "And I thank you for making me see that."

"You're welcome."

"But you've also made me see something else."

"That you want to get married." His voice was flat, emotionless.

"Yes. Or maybe I always knew that. Maybe that's why I became a wedding planner in the first place. I love it all—the flowers, the veil, the goddamn birdseed stuck in my hair. But mostly, I love the ritual. I love the standing together at the altar and pledging forever even though you know it might not work. I love the love."

"Love," Grant repeated, the word sounding like a foreign language tripping from his tongue.

"Love," Anna repeated, folding her arms over her chest to keep herself from shivering. "I want the whole package. Everything. The man, the emotion, the ceremony, the rings, the commitment, the legal bond, the happily ever after."

"I—I don't know what to say."

He looked like a trapped animal. Anna took a shaky breath and uncrossed her arms. "I'm not saying I need that with you. Just that I need someday, and that whoever I date needs to feel the same way." She stopped herself, then shook her head. "Hell, maybe I'm lying again."

She started to pace, raking her fingers through her hair as Grant sat silent. "Obviously, I don't expect any sort of commitment from you after a week. Christ, that would be insane."

"Insane," Grant repeated, his voice taking on a robotic quality now.

"But I'm saying I want it all. I want to get married. Not now, but someday. I *need* that."

She turned to look at him and her heart nearly broke in two. He was staring down at his hands, looking lost and wounded and so bewildered, Anna's chest ached.

When he looked up at her, his eyes were filled with apology. "I don't need that. Marriage, I mean. Not ever."

She nodded, her throat too tight to speak right away.

"I understand."

"I'm sorry."

"Me, too." She took a shaky breath, suddenly feeling very naked and vulnerable standing on a balcony in her bikini. "I think I'd better go now."

He blinked. "Anna, wait—"

But she didn't wait. She turned and sprinted through the house, grateful she'd left her purse on the counter and her rental car in his driveway. She twisted the front doorknob, feeling a moment of panic when it wouldn't turn.

She twisted the dead bolt, feeling like an inmate escaping as Grant's voice echoed behind her.

"Wait, Anna, don't go!"

She made it halfway to her car before the tears started to flow.

• • •

Janelle handed Anna another tissue and covered her sister's hand with her own.

"And then I just left," Anna concluded, smearing the tissue over her eyes and blowing her nose again. "Just got in my car and drove away with Grant standing there on his porch yelling after me."

Janelle shook her head. "That's the dumbest thing I've ever heard."

"I can't really blame him. I didn't give him a chance to—"

"Not Grant. *You*."

Anna blinked. "I'm sorry?"

"No, *I'm* sorry. I can't believe you didn't feel like you could tell me about running off to Vegas with a stranger. I would have supported you, honey."

"I know. I just felt so embarrassed."

"I understand. But we all make mistakes. You've seriously been wallowing in this blame over my marriage ending?"

"I'm your sister—*and* I'm a wedding planner. I should have seen the signs."

"That's bullshit." Janelle shook her head, her expression strangely fierce. "I don't know whether to hug you or strangle you. Anna, if you had the power to predict which marriages will fail and which ones won't, you'd never need to work another day in your life because everyone would be lining up at your doorstep for your psychic services."

"But I—"

"Enough!" Janelle snatched the soggy tissue from her hands and dropped it into the wastebasket before handing her a fresh one. "How many weddings have you planned in your career?"

"Three hundred and eighty-two," Anna said automatically, dabbing her eyes.

"And how many marriages have you, personally, had? Like actually walked all the way down the aisle and said 'I do' before going home to make a life together?"

"Janelle, I—"

"None. Zero, zip, nada." Janelle squeezed her hand. "You may be the older sister, but this is one area where I've got you beat in experience, so let me tell you something, sweetie—marriage is fucking hard work. Even when it's a good one and you're not fighting all the time or dredging up past grievances, it still takes a lot of work. Mom and Dad worked like hell at it, and yeah, having kids put a strain on it. But so did careers and mortgages and the fact that Mom wanted to travel and Dad liked to stay at home, and Dad enjoyed wine tasting while Mom couldn't stand it. Those were all factors, but you haven't spent your life boycotting jobs or real estate or vacations or Pinot Noir, have you?"

Anna wasn't sure what to say, so she just shook her head. "No." She looked down at the tissue, which she'd started to shred into soggy little ribbons. "The thing is, I was getting to this point already. The point of forgiving myself and realizing I didn't deserve a lifetime of punishing myself for bad decisions and other people's botched marriages. And I owe at least some of that to Grant."

"I know, honey. The man made you realize you wanted marriage and then ran like hell when he thought you might want it with him. I'll deal with him later."

"Please don't," Anna said, sniffling again. "It's not his fault. You don't go springing the M-word on a man when you've known each other ten days."

"Hmph," Janelle said, clearly not convinced, but spared from saying anything further by a knock at the door. She stood up and marched across the room to unfasten the dead bolt. She flung open the door, looking ready to spit nails.

"Speak of the devil," she said, pushing the door wider.

Anna looked up and felt the bottom fall out of her stomach. "Grant. What are you doing here?"

"You left before I got a chance to explain."

Anna shook her head, feeling like an idiot for sitting here sobbing over a man who didn't want to marry her.

Jesus. Talk about a stereotype.

"There's nothing to explain, Grant," she said, trying to keep her voice even and hoping her face wasn't blotchy and red. "It's fine. We have different goals in life, and that's okay. It was fun while it lasted, but there's no reason to shed any tears over it."

She forced herself to smile, a gesture that made her whole face feel prickly with dried tears. With a discreet sweep of her arm, she tried to push a pile of crumpled tissues into the wastebasket, along with four sticks from Fudgsicles she and Janelle had devoured in the last fifteen minutes.

God, you're pathetic.

She half expected him to run, but he just glanced at the wastebasket, then back at her. He met her eyes again, his expression pleading. "Can we go someplace and talk privately for a minute?"

"You can have this place to yourselves," Janelle said, not sounding too thrilled about it. "I have a manicure appointment in fifteen minutes anyway. Anna? Is that okay?"

Anna looked at Grant, then nodded at her sister. "Go. It's fine. Thank you for everything."

Janelle walked back over and gave her a sloppy hug. "Hear him out, okay?" Janelle whispered. "I'll cut his heart out later if I need to, but at least give him a chance to explain. The man rubbed papaya on your butt and rescued a cat from a tree. He deserves a chance to speak his mind."

Anna nodded and released her sister. Janelle grabbed her purse from the space next to the laptop on the kitchen table, then flounced out the door with one backward glance at Grant.

As soon as her footsteps faded away, Anna turned to

Grant. "And now you know."

"Know what?" He seemed to hesitate, then moved across the room and dropped heavily into the kitchen chair Janelle had vacated. He looked tired, and his shirt was wrinkled.

"Know I'm just like all the other girls. I fantasize about frilly dresses, I eat Fudgsicles when I'm sad, and I cry when I have my heart broken."

Grant winced, then leaned forward with his elbows on his knees. He sighed and put his head in his hands, looking down at the floor. "I'm sorry, Anna. I never meant for this to happen."

"It's not your fault. We were both up front with each other about not planning any sort of future that involved marriage. I'm the one who had a change of heart, not you."

He took a heavy breath, still not meeting her eyes. "I wish it didn't have to be like this."

Anna studied the back of his head. Her tears had dried up, and there was a prickle of something else in the back of her throat. If this thing between them was over before it even got started, at least she could get some answers. Some little shred of honesty from the man who'd been so hell-bent on hiding himself.

She rested her hand on the laptop, then flicked the power button with her index finger. Grant's flash drive was still in the USB port, and Anna slowly navigated her way to the folder.

"Grant?"

"Yeah?"

"When I got back here after leaving your place, I didn't want to come inside right away. I wasn't ready to face my sister, so I sat there in my car and looked up a word on my phone. Desiderium?"

He'd gone very, very still. He was still breathing, but other than that, he looked like a man frozen. Anna kept talking.

"It's Latin. There are a few different meanings, but the one that jumped out at me was 'grief, longing, or regret.'"

He said nothing, just sat there like a statue, so Anna went on. "I saw the photos on the drive. The pictures of your brother?"

It was an awkward subject change from their breakup to his family, but what the hell did she have to lose? If nothing else, she wanted answers. About Grant, about his secrets, about what on earth made him the way he was.

"Why don't you ever talk about your brother?" she asked. "What happened?"

He shook his head slowly, raising it up to look at the image splashed across the screen. He didn't look surprised to see it there. Just tired. So very, very tired.

"I can't—" He began, then stopped. He let out a heavy breath and looked away again. "I just can't."

"You can, actually. You just choose not to. You're willing to bare your body to me, but never your soul. Not what you're thinking or feeling, not ever. Why is that?"

He shook his head, but didn't speak, so Anna answered her own question.

"You're scared to death to let anyone see the real you. The you that isn't perfectly perfect all the time."

He shook his head, but didn't argue. Didn't defend himself.

"Okay, then how about another question," Anna tried. "If this is over between us, at least let me have the closure of some answers." When he didn't say anything, she licked her lips and continued. "Why don't you want to get married? I don't mean right now or to me. I mean ever. What's your reason for feeling like that?"

"I told you—"

"Actually, no. You didn't."

He looked up, his eyes dark gray and stormy. "Sure I did. We've talked about this stuff."

"No, *we* haven't. I've done all the talking. I've told you about my parents' divorce and my guilt over my sister's failed marriage and my stupid near miss in Vegas, while you used your supersecret spy-hunter skills to keep me sharing story after story after story. I'm not saying it's all your fault. I'm not exactly the kind of girl who keeps her thoughts to herself. But this whole time, you've hardly shared anything with me."

Grant looked at her for a moment, then glanced away. He didn't say anything, but Anna had a feeling she'd touched a nerve. She reached out and rested a hand on his arm. She hesitated a few beats, drawing out the silence the way he'd taught her in an interrogation.

Then she asked the one question she'd been wanting to ask all along.

"Who was she?"

She felt his whole body stiffen. When he looked back at her, his eyes were more troubled than she'd ever seen in her life.

He sighed and closed his eyes.

And then he began to talk.

Chapter Thirteen

Ten years ago

Grant walked into the bar, feeling the thrum of country music twanging through his veins. This wasn't his usual scene, but he was on vacation.

Most of the other bars he'd poked his head in had been teeming with military folks. Fort Irwin was home to the National Training Center where units came to get ready for overseas deployment. He'd seen a few of Schwartz's Army buddies at the last bar, and a couple of his fellow Marines down the street. Tonight though, Grant felt like trying something different.

"What can I getcha?" the bartender asked as Grant ambled over and straddled a stool.

"Whiskey and Coke," he said, pulling out his wallet to flash his ID before the bartender even asked. He'd just turned twenty-three but hadn't been able to lose the baby face. The bartender nodded, then thunked a smeared-looking glass down in front of him. He dropped in a couple ice cubes, then filled it halfway with cheap-looking whiskey.

The Coke seemed like an afterthought, but Grant thanked him anyway and shoved a twenty across the bar. The guy nodded and turned to the cash register.

"You stationed here?" the bartender asked.

Grant took a sip of the drink and tried not to choke. Schwartz always drank his whiskey straight, and so did Mac. How the fuck did they do it? Grant took another gulp and set the glass down. "Nah, I'm stationed over at Camp Twentynine Palms. I just drove over for the weekend to visit my brother. He's a trainer at the NTC. Staff sergeant. Runs all kinds of tactical training exercises for units that come here to certify." Grant realized he sounded boastful and also a little young, so he picked up his drink and took another sip. The bartender busied himself wiping down the bar with a damp rag, while Grant surveyed the room. It was oddly peaceful here. Two cowboys sat hunched together playing cards next to the jukebox, which was belting out a twangy tune about a dog and a truck.

In another corner, three women in cutoff shorts and halter tops sat giggling and sipping neon-colored drinks. One of them smiled at him, then leaned across the table to whisper to her friends. All of them turned to look at him, and for lack of anything better to do, Grant smiled.

"Your brother meeting you here?"

Grant turned back to the bartender. "Nah, my brother's out of town. I drove out here to surprise him, but it turns out he's in L.A. this weekend."

"Birthday?"

"Nope, he just got engaged. I got the call from him two nights ago. I haven't met her yet, so I thought I'd come out and offer my congratulations in person."

"That's mighty thoughtful of you."

Grant nodded and turned at the sound of female giggles. One of the women from the corner—the one who'd pointed at him—was making her way toward him, a sexy sway in her hips. It didn't take much to figure she'd put it there for him.

Grant waited, pretty sure she looked like trouble, but not having anything better to do at the moment.

"Hey, soldier," she said, sliding onto the barstool next to his. "Buy me a drink?"

"I'm actually a Marine, not a soldier," he said, then smiled to show he wasn't a total asshole. He glanced back at her table and noticed she already had a drink, but it didn't seem polite to point that out. She'd undone an extra button on her top, so it seemed rude not to show some appreciation.

"What do you want to drink?"

"Tequila sunrise. Extra cherry."

Grant nodded at the bartender, who turned around and began making the drink. The woman leaned close and extended her hand. "Jenny," she said. "You have the most beautiful gray eyes."

"Thank you, Jenny. I'm Grant. Grant Patton. And you have the most beautiful—"

She shifted a little on her barstool then, making everything jiggle and distracting him for an instant. He suspected it wasn't an accident. "Eyes," he said at last. "You have beautiful eyes, too."

She laughed like he'd said the funniest thing in the world. She reached for her drink as the bartender set it in front of her. "Grant Patton," she said. "What's a nice guy like you doing in a seedy bar like this?"

The bartender grunted a little at that, but said nothing. Grant sipped his drink again. Was it his imagination, or had Jenny just undone another button on her shirt?

"Just in town visiting for the weekend," he said.

"Vacation?"

"Something like that."

She smiled and leaned closer. He could feel the heat from her skin, smelled something soft and floral. It had been a couple months, and Grant felt his cock lunge at the sight of all that flesh on display.

Jenny sipped her drink again, looking at him over the straw. "Vacations are all about having a good time. Wouldn't you say?"

Grant didn't say much over the course of the next twenty minutes. Jenny did all the talking, including making the suggestion they head back to his hotel room. Grant raised no objections, though he did ask once if she was positive she hadn't had too much tequila.

"Relax, sweetie," she'd said with a laugh, grabbing his arm as he led her back to the hotel.

When it was all over, Jenny swung her bare legs over the edge of the bed and began rummaging around on the floor for her shirt. "I've gotta run, baby. Thanks for the good time."

He watched her get dressed, feeling a little disoriented. He'd had casual flings before, but none quite this casual. He sat up with the sheets still tangled around his waist, wondering if he should offer to call a cab. No, that would be stupid. She'd told him she only lived three blocks away.

"Should I, uh, call you later?"

She rolled her eyes and stuffed her feet into her abandoned flip-flops. "Under the circumstances, that would be pretty stupid, don't you think?"

Grant opened his mouth to answer, but Jenny cut him off.

"Don't bother. This was fantasy fodder, nothing more. You and your brother are remarkably similar in bed, you know that? I'll be thinking of that next spring as I'm walking down the aisle to marry him."

And with that, she turned and flounced out of the room.

• • •

"Oh my God."

The stricken look on Anna's face felt like a sucker punch right in Grant's solar plexus. It was like reliving that moment all over again, only this time, he had an audience.

She shook her head, looking too horrified for words. Grant swallowed and looked down at his hands.

"Schwartz found out, of course. I'm not sure how, but I suspect it was one of Jenny's friends. Or hell, maybe the bartender. I never knew, exactly. Just got an email from Schwartz saying, 'Jenny cheated, the engagement's off.'"

"Did he—do you think—"

"Did he know it was me?" Grant balled his hands into fists. "I never knew. I don't think so, but I can't be sure. A week later, he volunteered to join a unit deploying to Anbar Provence. It was crazy. Schwartz was a tactical-operations trainer for the Army. He did predeployment training. He was a badass, sure, but he wasn't supposed to head into the danger zone. Not then, anyway. Not when things were heating up down there."

Anna was shaking her head. "You think he was so upset by what happened—"

"I don't just think. I *know*. He talked to Mac the night before he left and said all this shit about needing to get away, to go where the action was." Grant took another deep breath, bracing himself for the worst part of the story. "Nine months later, his Humvee was hit by a rocket. Everyone but Schwartz was killed, and he was pretty messed up. When he came back, nothing was the same. He wanted nothing to do with anyone—not the family, not the military, definitely not women. He wanted to be left alone. For good. That's what he said."

"And you obliged?"

There was a note of dismay in her voice, but Grant chose to ignore it. "I tried at first to stay in touch. I'm the only one he trusted with his contact info, and for a while I thought that meant something. But no matter how many ways I tried, he shut me out. He told me to leave him the hell alone, and so I did."

He watched Anna's throat move as she swallowed. When she reached out to touch his arm, her hand was warm and soft and filled with a tenderness he didn't deserve.

"Grant, it wasn't your fault."

He shook his head, hating the sympathy in her voice almost as much as he hated the pity in her eyes.

Not nearly as much as he hated himself, though.

"Are you kidding me? Of course it was my fault. I slept with my brother's fiancée, broke his goddamn heart, and sent him careening into a combat zone where he didn't fucking belong. You want to tell me how that's not my fault?"

She jerked back a little at the force of his words, but her hand didn't leave his arm. She shook her head, tears clouding her eyes now as a look of determination crossed her face. "No. You couldn't have known who she was, Grant."

He shook his head slowly. He knew the instant the words left his mouth that nothing would be the same again. That she'd take her hand off his arm and everything would change between them.

But still, he had to say it.

"No," he said, forcing himself to meet her eyes. Those beautiful, trusting eyes he'd give anything to gaze into for the rest of his life.

But that would never happen. "You don't understand," he said at last. "I knew exactly who she was."

Chapter Fourteen

Anna blinked, wondering if she'd misunderstood. "I'm sorry?"

"You heard me right," he said, pulling his arm back so her hand slipped off and bounced awkwardly off his knee. "I knew Jenny was Schwartz's fiancée and I slept with her anyway."

He stood up then, not meeting her eyes. "I'm sorry, Anna. I'm not the man you thought I was."

She let those words hang there between them for a moment before she stood up, too. "When?"

"It happened ten years ago."

"No, not that. You already said that. I mean when did you know she was his fiancée? At the bar? Before you even got down there?"

"Why does it matter?"

"I'm trying to understand."

He sighed and raked his hands over his buzz cut. "Not until we were back at the hotel and—uh—already to third base. I made a crack about not being the sort of guy to sleep with someone if I didn't even know her full name, and she just laughed."

"She laughed?"

"Then she slid down on her knees and—" He closed his eyes, unable to finish the sentence.

So Anna gave it her best shot. "Told you with your cock in her mouth that she planned to marry your brother? Is that about it?"

Grant gave a tight nod, but said nothing.

Anna grabbed his arm and dug her nails in, forcing him to look at her. "Let me get this straight. You were a twenty-three-year-old kid with a raging case of hero worship for your brother, and you found yourself unable to resist when his fiancée—who obviously set the whole thing up—took off her clothes, took your dick in her mouth, and asked you to fuck her?"

"Please don't."

"The hell I won't!" Anna snapped, leaping to her feet. "We all make mistakes, Grant. Even perfect Boy Scouts like you. You sure as hell insisted I stop blaming myself for mine. What makes you any less worthy of redemption?"

He shook his head, looking tired and beaten down and desperate to be anywhere but here. "It's not that simple, Anna. My brother's life was ruined because of me."

"Even if that were true—which I don't believe for an instant—you're going to punish yourself forever by never allowing yourself to marry and be happy?"

Something flickered in his eyes. "Isn't that exactly what you've been doing?"

Anna blinked, startled. "You're right. It is. But you know what, Grant? I talk about my feelings. I share my regrets and fears and hang-ups, and thanks to you, I was even figuring out how to learn from my mistakes. You were the one who told me not to spend the rest of my life in purgatory. Why the hell can't you do the same for yourself?"

He shook his head. "Three months. Schwartz was in a coma for *three fucking months*. He was hospitalized a lot longer than that. They had to completely rebuild his leg. Physical therapy, psychotherapy. Then there was the rest of my family. You should have seen what it did to my mother—" His voice broke there, and Anna felt her heart split in two. She wanted to put her arms around him and tell him everything would be okay, but Grant had already turned away from her. "Some people don't deserve forgiveness, Anna."

"That's where you're wrong, Grant. So very, very wrong."

"One of countless reasons I'd be a terrible husband to anyone." He began moving toward the door, his steps stiff and halting. At the threshold, he hesitated and looked over his shoulder at her, his eyes so stormy they were nearly black. "I'm sorry, Anna."

Anna folded her arms over her chest, torn between anger, heartache, and plain old frustration.

"Being a good partner isn't about never being wrong, Grant. It's about being able to admit when you are. It's about learning from it and moving on. You are more than the worst thing you've done, Grant Patton."

But he was already out the door, and out of Anna's life for good.

• • •

Grant didn't know how he ended up on the beach. He had no recollection of getting in his car and driving, though he must have driven quite a distance to have ended up here on Pakala.

"Cow Beach" his sister called it, naming it for the pack of bovines that occasionally wandered out of the jungle to sun themselves on the sand.

But there were no cows now, and no sun, for that matter. Inky clouds choked off the sky, and a fierce wind was whipping the palm trees into a frenzy.

Grant toed off his shoes under a piece of driftwood and began walking. When that pace proved inadequate to outrace his thoughts, he began to run. He ran until his legs burned, until he dripped with sweat and his legs were covered in a fine sheen of sand.

He might have run forever if his phone hadn't rung. He pulled it out of his pocket, frowning at the sweat-fogged glass. This was why he normally ran with an armband. What the hell was it with his phone ringing every time he went for a run?

You run when you're scared, and lately you've been running a helluva lot.

He brushed off the screen, but the readout just said "blocked." He considered ignoring it, but Mac often called from secure lines. If there was a family emergency—

"Hello?"

"Grant."

It came out more like a grunt than a name, but Grant would have recognized that grunt anywhere.

"Schwartz. What—did she call you?"

"She who?"

"Anna."

"What the hell are you talking about? Who the fuck is Anna?"

He realized in an instant what a dumb thing he'd asked, but he'd been harboring the fantasy anyway. That somehow, Anna would know how to reach his brother. That she'd explain the whole goddamn mess, somehow making everything right between them.

But that was absurd. No one but him even knew how to reach Schwartz, and there was no reason for Anna to try anyway.

"Never mind," he said, gripping the phone tighter. "You're returning my call. About coming to Sheri's wedding."

"Right," he grunted. "You know I don't do weddings. Or birthdays. Or baby showers. Or—"

"Civilization in general," Grant finished. "I know. I just thought maybe—I don't know. That you'd make an exception. For Sheri."

Schwartz was quiet on the other end of the line. For a moment, Grant wondered if he'd hung up.

"What the hell is wrong with you?" he demanded.

Grant frowned. "What do you mean?"

"That probably came out wrong." Schwartz fell quiet again. "I mean you sound upset, is everything okay?"

"Right." Grant took a shaky breath. "Apparently I'm emotionally unavailable and closed-off."

"They make pills for that shit, don't they?"

Grant closed his eyes and took a deep breath. It was now or never, goddammit. "I need to tell you something, Schwartz."

"Yeah?"

"It's about Jenny."

"Jenny who?"

Grant sighed, dragged his hand down his face. "Your

former fiancée? The one whose betrayal made you volunteer for deployment to Anbar Provence and sent your whole life spiraling down a path of desperation and despair."

"Have you been watching *Oprah*?"

"*Oprah's* not on the air anymore." Grant winced. "I'm ashamed that I know that. I was babysitting the twins for Sheri one afternoon and I saw the final show and—never mind, this is beside the point."

"What the fuck is your point?"

"It was me." The second the words were out of his mouth, Grant wanted to slam his head against the nearest palm tree. Instead, he kept going. "I was the one she cheated with, Schwartz. We met in a bar when I came out to surprise you, and one thing led to another and—"

"Why are you telling me this shit?"

"Because you deserve to know. Because I deserve whatever punishment you want to dole out."

There was a moment of silence on the other end of the line, and Grant realized how frantic he'd sounded just then. Christ, he wouldn't blame Schwartz for hanging up on him. He deserved a helluva lot worse.

"You always did have a flair for the drama, little brother."

Grant swallowed. "What?"

"I already knew all this shit, Grant. And that Joni—"

"Jenny."

"Whatever the fuck her name was," Schwartz growled, "was a scheming tramp I didn't think twice about once she packed up her shit and left."

Grant froze, digesting his brother's words. "You're lying."

"Why the fuck would I lie about that?"

"How did you—Why did you—What the—"

"What's the question, Grant?"

He honestly didn't know. He sat down on a piece of drift-wood as the rain started spattering into the sand around him. He barely noticed. "I don't understand. I ruined your life."

"You think my life is ruined?" He sounded bemused.

"No. I mean, yes. Having your whole team blown to bits right in front of you?"

There was an odd growl on the other end of the line. "Did you fire the fucking rocket that hit us?"

"No."

"Did you start the goddamn war?"

"No, but—"

"Did you choose to raise me in a strict military family where we were pretty much expected to join up the minute we got big enough to lift an assault rifle?"

"What? Are you saying it's Mom and Dad's fault?"

"No, you idiot. I'm saying it's no one's fault. I wanted to see some action, so I went where the action was. I wanted to serve my goddamn country, so I did. I knew the risks, and I did it anyway because it's what I wanted to do. None of it had anything to do with you or Mom or Dad or Jessie—"

"Jenny."

"Whatever," Schwartz said. "Is this conversation almost over?"

"Wait. So you don't hate me?"

"Hate you? Of course not, you dumbshit. I love you."

Tears pricked the back of Grant's eyes, or maybe it was just the sting of windswept sand hitting his face. He wiped a smear of rain off his face and pressed the phone harder against his ear. "That's the nicest thing anyone's ever said to me."

"In that case, you seriously need to find a woman."

"I did," Grant muttered. "And then I fucked it up."

"Well go unfuck it then."

"How?"

"What am I, your fucking shrink? How the hell should I know? Buy her some beer or flowers or some shit like that."

"How is it you're still single?"

Schwartz made a sound that was almost a laugh, or as close to a laugh as the grumpy bastard could ever get.

"I really am sorry about what happened to you," Grant said. "About Jenny and the accident and the fact that you live in the middle of nowhere with no one to keep you warm at night."

"Jesus, dude. You're seriously starting to depress me. Go get your woman and leave me the hell alone."

"I love you, too, man."

Schwartz grunted in reply, and before Grant could say anything else, he heard his brother's line go dead. He stared at the phone for a minute, then put it back in his pocket.

"That was a beautiful Hallmark moment."

Grant whirled around to see Mac standing behind him under a large palm tree. "Where the hell did you come from?"

"I followed you."

Grant stood up, dusting the sand off his shorts. "You know, sometimes you're downright creepy."

"My wife says the same thing. I think she finds it charming."

"Yeah, well, your brother finds it disturbing."

"Speaking of brothers, it sounds like you've connected with ours."

"What did you do, bug my phone?"

Mac didn't answer, and Grant tried to decide how annoyed to be about that. He was saved from deciding when Mac folded his arms over his chest and stared him down.

"Do you remember what you said to me several months ago when I was behaving in a fashion that was not conducive to a positive romantic relationship?"

"I told you to pull your head out of your ass."

"In a manner of speaking. And while I prefer to think I'm more refined than to offer that precise bit of advice, I'd like to invite you to do the same. Promptly, I should add."

Grant sighed and dragged his hands down his face. "You talked to Anna?"

"No. I talked to our mother, who'd spoken with Sheri, who'd talked with Kelli during her dinner break. I would have gotten the news directly from my wife, but I prefer not to visit when she's in the middle of neutering cats."

"I can't imagine why."

"In any case, it sounds like you have problems."

"And I suppose you plan to tell me how to solve them?"

Mac frowned. "Good God, no. I'm just here to tell you we have a tux fitting at 8:00 a.m."

"You stalked me on an isolated beach to tell me that?"

Mac shook his head and pulled off his sunglasses, and Grant had a rare glimpse of his brother's steely brown eyes. "Don't fuck this up, Grant. I don't know what all your demons are, but I know it gets a lot easier to fight them when you're no longer doing battle alone."

"Meaning what?"

"Meaning women have much bigger swords than you might imagine," he said. "Now go make sure she doesn't use hers on you."

Chapter Fifteen

"I need to state, for the record, that I wouldn't ordinarily give a client a bridal-shower gift with penises printed on the wrapping paper," Anna said as she handed the package to Sheri. "Kelli insisted."

As Anna kissed the bride-to-be on the cheek, Kelli beamed with pride. "I also insisted on a naughty-or-nice theme for the shower, but I may have forgotten to include the nice part. You're welcome."

Sheri laughed and hugged them both. "I don't know what I'd do without you two."

"You'd have an embarrassingly small collection of sex toys," Kelli supplied. "Again, I say you're welcome. Come on already, start opening the damn gifts."

The thirty or so women attending the shower had arranged themselves in a sort of lopsided circle of folding chairs. Most balanced dainty slices of cake on paper plates, and nearly everyone held a champagne flute. It had been a good party so far, with lots of laughing and good food and happy congratulations for the bride. Anna smiled, grateful she'd been able to go with the flow despite feeling like her heart had been smooshed like a glob of frosting in the tines of a plastic fork. She had to put on a happy face for the bride. Just a few more days and she could fly home to Portland and forget about Grant and his brother and the whole damn Patton family.

Fat chance.

Sheri took her seat in a spot near the window flanked by her mother and Kelli. Anna stationed herself in the corner near the kitchen so she could help refill champagne glasses and gather discarded gift bows to make a bouquet for the rehearsal the next night.

Sheri spotted her and frowned, then waved her over. "Come on, Anna. Don't stand there like you're the hired help."

"I am the hired help."

"The last hired help in my life is set to be my husband in a few days," Sheri said. "The Patton family takes a different view of the concept. We're practically family, Anna. Come on." She pointed to the empty chair beside Kelli. "Sit with us. That way we can all drink too much champagne and discuss what an ass-hat my brother is."

"For the last time, your brother's not an ass-hat," Anna said as she trudged over to Sheri's side of the room. She glanced around at the assembled women, most of whom were total strangers. She leaned down to Sheri and lowered her voice. "Can we please not make a public spectacle of the fact that I hooked up with your brother? It's unprofessional."

"Honey, please," Kelli said. "Half the women in this

room would give their left nipple to bang Grant, and the other half would give up their right. No one's blaming you for falling."

"It's okay, Anna, I understand," Sheri said, touching her arm. "I'll stop bringing it up. I'm sorry."

"Come on, let's distract you with sex stuff," Kelli said, reaching into the pile of gifts at Sheri's feet.

"Sex stuff," Anna said. "Always a good distraction."

Sheri bent down to inspect the packages. "Should I open the one that looks like it's filled with slutty lingerie, or the one that feels like an exceptionally heavy sex toy?"

"Sex toy," Anna said, dropping into the empty chair and pulling out a notepad and her favorite clicky pen. "I'll start a tally of how many batteries you'll need."

At the thought of batteries, Anna felt a pang of nostalgia. Christ, this was stupid. She'd only spent a week with Grant, and already she had tainted memories of batteries, coleslaw, and paddleboarding. Good thing the relationship hadn't lasted longer or she wouldn't have been left with much that didn't remind her of him.

"Oooooh!" Kelli cried as Sheri tore the wrapping paper off the first package. "A spinning sex swing. Those are much sturdier than the kind you mount in a doorway."

"We went in on it together," called a perky-looking brunette across the room. "That's from all the Patton cousins."

"A little different from the playground equipment we enjoyed together when we were eight," Sheri said, turning the box over in her hands. "Thank you so much."

"You need to pass the gifts around, dear," Stella said beside her. "That's the proper etiquette."

"I wasn't aware there was etiquette involved in allowing

thirty of my closest friends and family members to fondle my sex toys," Sheri said, but passed the box toward her mother anyway.

She reached for another box, this one small and rectangular. Some sort of lingerie, Anna guessed, and watched as Sheri unwrapped a surprisingly tasteful white teddy.

Anna felt a stupid pang of jealousy and then wanted to kick herself. Would she ever have the chance to rip pink paper off tasteless gifts while her doting husband-to-be gathered with his buddies at a tuxedo shop in the days before their wedding? She thought about Grant trying on his tux and somehow the thoughts got all mixed up in her mind with Grant standing at the altar beaming while she floated down the aisle toward him.

Stop it, she commanded herself. *Just because it'll never be Grant doesn't mean it won't be anyone.*

"I don't want just anyone."

She must have murmured it under her breath, because Kelli turned to look at her. "I hear you, sister. That's one thing you can say for the Patton men. They're not your average everyman."

"Thank you, dear," Stella said from the opposite side of Sheri, leaving Anna wondering if the woman had radar hearing. She wondered what else she knew about what had happened between her and Grant. Anna hadn't meant to spill the whole story to Kelli on the phone a few days ago, but once she had, she'd felt better.

"Is this top secret?" Kelli had asked her. "My lips are sealed if it is."

"You can tell Sheri if you want," Anna said. "Discreetly, I mean. That way everything's out in the open and there's no awkwardness. I want the focus of the party to be on Sheri instead of the tramp who shagged her brother."

Not that she didn't feel awkward anyway, Anna thought now as she watched Sheri hand a pair of edible panties to her mother. She jotted the gift down on her notepad, along with the fact that it came from one of Sam's sisters.

"Open that one next," Kelli insisted, picking up an oblong box. "I think I heard it buzzing earlier."

Anna busied herself jotting notes, making sure to provide enough detail to help Sheri write good thank-you notes later. She looked up every now and then when Kelli murmured something appreciative like, "that's a huge one" or "the strawberry flavor is the best," but mostly she kept her eyes on her notes as the wrapping paper piled up at her feet.

"Excuse me, Anna?"

Anna turned to the woman on her right, who held out an armload of sex toys and lingerie. "Sorry, I didn't want to bother you while you were busy taking notes, but we're backing up here."

"I'm so sorry," she said, tucking her pen into the coiled spine of her notepad. She held out her arms to accept the world's largest assortment of sex paraphernalia. Lubes, crotchless teddies, vibrating panties—all of it toppled into Anna's lap. She wrapped her arms around the pile, shifting her notebook to her knee. She glanced over at Sheri to see if the bride was blushing.

"Ohmygod, I've wanted one of these!" The bride held up a dildo shaped like a handgun, not a trace of embarrassment on her face.

"You're welcome, dear," Stella said beside her. "Kelli helped me choose it."

"Of course she did," Anna murmured, struggling to wrestle her pen free as she juggled the giant armload of sex toys.

Somewhere in the distance, a male voice echoed in a hallway.

"Anna? Anna, are you here?"

She tried to scramble to her feet, but she couldn't do it without sending a mountain of sex paraphernalia tumbling to the floor. An instant later, Grant was standing in the doorway looking flushed and disheveled in a tuxedo. He was gripping a bouquet of sunflowers in one hand and something that looked like a cupcake in the other.

"Anna," he said again, relief washing over his features before turning to mild confusion as he surveyed her armload of booty. He shook his head and drew his eyes back to hers, a look of determination on his face. "I need to talk to you."

"Does that vibrate?" Kelli asked, squinting at the cupcake.

"It's orange ginger with lavender-lemon icing," Grant said, not really answering the question, but thrusting it toward Anna anyway. "I had it custom-made."

Anna shook her head, wishing the ground would swallow her up. "Grant! What are you doing? You can't be here, you'll ruin the bride's party."

Sheri raised her hand and leaned across Kelli so she was practically in Anna's lap.

Not that there was any room left.

"As the bride, I'd like to disagree." Sheri smiled at Grant. "The floor is yours, baby brother. This better be good."

Anna watched Grant survey the surrounding army of women in pastel dresses. Every one of them had stopped talking to stare at them. Most looked curious or mildly amused. Some wore expressions of hunger, though most weren't looking at the cupcake.

She saw Grant draw his eyes back to her and take a steadying breath. He stepped forward, still gripping the flowers and the cupcake. She was eye level with his crotch now, which must have felt as awkward for him as it did for her, because he hesitated, then dropped to his knees in front of her.

"Grant, no. Get up, please—"

"No," he said, his eyes still locked on hers. "It may not be today or tomorrow or even the next day, but someday—hopefully very soon—I plan to get down on one knee and ask the woman I love to marry me. And I *do* love you, Anna. I'm not making any promises right now, except that I love you."

A symphony of gasps echoed in the room, and Anna realized at least one of them came from her. She tried to raise a hand to her mouth, but discovered she was still gripping a bottle of flavored massage oil.

Grant didn't seem to notice. "I love you," he repeated. "And I want to thank you for opening my eyes to the fact that I want it all—the wife, the home, the happy marriage—the whole goddamn mess."

Anna blinked back tears, not sure how the man managed to make a goddamn mess sound romantic, but he was doing a damn fine job of it.

And of filling out the tux. She blinked again, trying to stay focused on his words.

"Look, Anna. When I told you I wasn't perfect, I meant it. I told you I'm stubborn as hell, but that means I'm willing to fight for what I want. I'm clueless about things like fashion and home decor, but when I pull my head out of my ass I've usually got a pretty clear view of other things. Like the fact that I've got an amazing woman right here in front of me." He swallowed, his voice still a little shaky. "I know I told you I care too much what people think of me, and it's true. But I care most of all what you think of me, and I want to be worthy of your love and respect. I'm willing to learn from you, Anna—your bluntness and your honesty and your ability to grow as a person. I want you to teach me, whether it's how to tell a Pinot Noir from a Cherry Coke, or how to be emotionally available. Please, Anna, say you'll give me a chance."

She couldn't seem to find any words, but she managed to nod as tears welled in her eyes. Grant smiled and pressed on.

"You deserve sunflowers and orange-ginger cupcakes with lavender-lemon icing. You deserve the damn tea-length dress and whatever the hell a mantilla veil is. But most of all, you deserve happiness, Anna. Let me be the one to give it to you."

She still couldn't find her voice, but she'd given up blinking back the tears. They were rolling down her face in earnest now, making big, soggy droplets on her notepad.

Stella seemed to notice, and leaned across her daughter to reach for the paper. "I'll take that," she said, tugging the pen and notepad from her fingers as Anna sat numbly. She glanced at Stella's face to see her smiling proudly at her son.

"And I'll take those," Kelli said, scooping the armload of sex paraphernalia from Anna's lap.

Sheri leaned forward and plucked the cupcake and flowers from her brother's hands. "And I'll take these."

"And I'll take you," Anna said, sliding to her knees on the floor in front of Grant as she found her words at last. "All of you. The flaws and the perfection and everything in between. I love all of you, Grant. And I don't need you to promise to marry me. Just the possibility it *could* happen is enough."

"It could," he said, his hands sliding around her back to pull her tight against him. "It definitely could."

"Stranger things have happened," Anna murmured as his lips found hers.

Behind her, Stella began to laugh. "In this family? You're barely getting started."

• • •

Grant slid a finger into the collar of his tuxedo shirt and gave a little tug to adjust it.

"Bow tie too tight?" Mac murmured beside him.

Grant shook his head and grinned, feeling himself breathe easy. "Nope. It's just right."

The pianist was playing loudly enough to cover their whispers, but Sam glanced over anyway and made a pistol with his thumb and forefinger. Both Mac and Grant saluted him, and Sam grinned, then turned his attention back to the doors of the church. The procession had begun.

Grant watched his new brother-in-law visibly swell with pride as Sam's stepmom and Stella Patton moved down the aisle shoulder to shoulder, each carrying one of Sheri's twin boys. Spotting Sam at the front of the church, Jackson hooted and waved a chubby fist in the air, while Jeffrey shouted something Grant could've sworn sounded like, "Semper Fi."

Grant glanced at Mac, who looked pleased with himself.

"You taught them that before they mastered bye-bye?" Grant murmured.

"Shh!" Sam hissed.

The moms took their seats, making way for a parade of flower girls and bridesmaids in brightly colored dresses. Then it was time for the maid of honor.

The instant Kelli came through the church doors, Grant felt Mac stand taller beside him, his eyes locked on his wife's beaming face. She spotted her husband and blew him a kiss, looking radiant in a bright coral gown with flowers in her hair.

But Grant's eyes had already drifted to the edge of the door where he could see Anna hovering outside. She was issuing cues, directing traffic, the whole time smiling like a kid at a carnival. She was in her element, and he felt so damn proud to be part of it.

"You don't have to keep telling me you want to get married someday," she'd murmured against his chest, snuggling into his bed after the rehearsal dinner last night. "I believe you. I don't expect forever after less than two weeks."

He'd planted a kiss along her hairline and stroked his hand down her bare back. "I know. It just feels good to say it. No matter what happens."

But he knew what was going to happen. He was going to marry Anna someday, dammit.

A rustle in the crowd drew his focus back to the church doors. Everyone in the audience stood, and Grant straightened a little as his sister began a slow march down the aisle. She looked beautiful in a shimmery gown Anna had called "eggshell," whatever the hell that meant. The same curls

Grant used to tug as a little kid were pinned up under a fluffy-looking veil. Her cheeks were flushed and her shoulders were bare, and she was smiling at Sam like he was the best thing she'd ever seen in her life.

"Good God," Sam murmured beside him, and Grant smiled to see his new brother-in-law staring at her in wonder.

Sheri smiled and walked toward him, her eyes shimmering with emotion. She reached her groom's side and stood on tiptoe to kiss him.

"You're skipping ahead a little," Grant whispered.

"It's my wedding," she whispered. "I can do whatever the hell I want."

"Indeed," Mac agreed, nodding over Grant's shoulder.

"You look beautiful," Sam murmured, and Grant took a step back to give them a moment of privacy. He looked away, his eyes scanning the crowd for Anna. He spotted her near the doorway, her eyes fixed on the happy couple. She was beaming with joy, her red hair glistening in the sunlight that filtered through the windows. She wore a blue dress, and though she'd tastefully pinned her hair behind her ears, Grant could still see the blue streak peeking through the coppery strands.

Grant caught her eye and smiled. *You look beautiful*, he mouthed. *I love you.*

She smiled back. *I love you, too.*

He forced himself to look away. This was his sister's big day, and he didn't want to detract from that by ogling the wedding planner. There'd be plenty of time for that later.

He let his gaze drift across the crowd. There were a lot of people here, some cousins and aunts and uncles he recognized, and a few of Sam's sisters and a lot of assorted friends.

He spotted Janelle on the far side of the church and watched her hand a cable to the videographer. The man nodded and Janelle scurried discreetly out the side door, as unobtrusive as possible.

"Dearly beloved," the minister began, and Grant started to pull his eyes back to the happy couple.

He froze.

His eyes caught a flash of movement beyond the side door. A figure stood outside, cloaked in shadows, watching through the small sliver of light.

"We are gathered here this day to join this man and this woman in the bonds of holy matrimony."

Grant forced himself to pay attention, ignoring the prickle of unease in his gut. His sister was beaming at Sam now, reciting vows the two had written together.

"Through diapers and deployments, though burned dinners and good wine, I promise to love you—"

Grant swallowed back a lump in his throat as his sister and Sam took turns pledging their eternal devotion to one another. He couldn't ask for a better man to be marrying his sister, and he knew Sam was getting a helluva woman with Sheri. The service continued, and Grant stole another glance at the door. It wasn't ajar anymore, so maybe he'd been imagining things.

"I now pronounce you husband and wife," the minister said at last. "You may kiss the bride."

The audience erupted into applause, and Grant joined the cacophony. He clapped Sam on the back, and Mac followed suit.

"Congratulations, man. Take good care of her."

"Way to go, bro."

The happy couple didn't stop kissing, and Grant saw Anna beaming at the back of the church. He smiled at her, and she waved back. Her eyes looked glittery, and he wondered if she felt moved by the ceremony or by something else.

He kinda hoped it was a little of both.

As the pianist played the final bars of the song Grant only knew as "There Goes the Bride," his sister and Sam marched hand in hand down the aisle, laughing as each of them stopped to scoop up one of the twins. They headed toward the door, Sheri's veil trailing behind them on the breeze.

The crowd began to disperse, picking up purses and murmuring to each other about the vows and the flowers.

"So pretty."

"A wonderful couple."

"Such a lovely ceremony."

Grant made his way through the crowd, wondering when the day would come for his family and Anna's to gather together and murmur the same things about the two of them.

"You did a wonderful job," one of Sam's sisters was saying as she clasped Anna's hand. "Such a beautiful wedding. Do you have a card? My best friend is getting married next year, and she's been looking to hire someone."

"Of course," Anna said, beaming. "I left my purse in the other room, but I'll come find you at the reception."

"Fabulous," the woman said, and walked away.

"You're a popular woman," Grant said, sliding an arm around Anna as he stepped into the space the woman had vacated. "I don't suppose I could hire you?"

"I'm pretty sure there are laws against hiring people for

what you have in mind," she said, stretching up on tiptoe to kiss him. "I'm happy to volunteer, though."

"Your duties will be pretty extensive," he murmured, kissing her back. "Speaking of duties, I had a message from my command this morning."

"Oh?"

"There's a special intelligence project I'll be working on for PACOM. It's based out of Fort Lewis."

Anna's eyes went wide. Grant wasn't sure how to read her at first, but her smile was quick to alleviate his worry. "In Washington? That's only a couple hours from Portland."

"I know." Grant grinned and pulled her closer, pleased she seemed delighted instead of freaked out by how quickly things were moving. "We'll be able to see each other all the time."

"All the time," she repeated settling into his arms in a way that left him feeling certain she was made to fit there. "I can live with that."

Grant breathed in the flowery scent of her hair, feeling damn glad to be there, even if he did have to wear a monkey suit. Anna was soft and warm in his arms, and her cheek fit perfectly into the hollow of his chest.

He glanced back at the side door, surprised to see it ajar again.

A man stood in the shadows wearing a dark gray suit. He had a thick beard and dark sunglasses that weren't necessary in the dim light of the hall. Grant blinked. The man was watching him.

The figure moved a fraction of an inch, his body hidden almost completely by the door. A sliver of light fell across his face, and Grant froze.

Schwartz?

Even through the sunglasses, he could tell the man's eyes had locked with his. They stood frozen like that for a moment, neither of them moving or speaking or even seeming to breathe. Grant didn't blink. He couldn't tear his eyes from the space, couldn't stop his mind from racing to the possibility that his long-lost brother had decided to come after all.

Anna stirred in his arms. "We should probably get going to the reception," she murmured against his chest. "I want to get there before the caterer does."

Grant blinked. Through the sliver of light in the doorway, he saw the man turn away.

As the figure made his way down the hall, Grant saw the faintest trace of a limp.

Then the man was gone, vanished into the sunlight far away from the bustling crowd.

Acknowledgments

Tremendous thanks, as always, to Michelle Wolfson of Wolfson Literary. I'm forever grateful to have you in my corner, especially since our corner has all the good candy and beer.

Thank you to Heather Howland for being a kick-ass editor and all around awesome idea generator. I'm also grateful to the entire Entangled team for the fabulous support, promotion, distribution, and everything else you do to turn my words into books instead of crossword puzzles.

Big huge thank yous and sloppy hugs to "Major Sexypants" Jason Faler for all your help nailing down the military details. I couldn't have done this without your wisdom and insight, and any errors here are entirely my fault. Or my cats' fault. It's easier to blame them.

Thanks a million to my fabulous critique partners and beta readers, Linda Grimes, Cynthia Reese, Linda Brundage, Bridget McGinn, Minta Powelson, and Larie Borden. You ladies are my rock stars, only without the big hair and coke habit.

Oodles of gratitude to Aaron and Carlie Fenske for getting hitched on Kauai so I had an excuse to set a wedding-themed book there. Thanks also to my parents, David and Dixie Fenske, for choosing to live half the year on the island so I'll never run out of reasons to visit and use the locale as the setting for stories.

Thank you to Cedar and Violet for being the best step kids in several galaxies, and for continuing to be impressed by the sight of my books on store shelves.

And thanks especially to my husband (HUSBAND!), Craig Zagurski, for your endless support and love, and for the secret behind *that* scene.

About the Author

Tawna Fenske traveled a career path that took her from newspaper reporter to English teacher in Venezuela to marketing geek to PR manager for her city's tourism bureau. An avid globetrotter and social media fiend, Tawna is the author of the popular blog, Don't Pet Me, I'm Writing, and a member of Romance Writers of America. She lives with her gentleman friend in Bend, Oregon, where she'll invent any excuse to hike, bike, snowshoe, float the river, or sip beer along the Bend Ale Trail. She's published several romantic comedies with Sourcebooks, including *Making Waves* and *Believe it or Not*, as well as the interactive fiction caper, *Getting Dumped*, with Coliloquy.

Discover the **Front and Center** *series...*

MARINE FOR HIRE

Sam Kercher is every inch a wickedly hot Marine. But when his best friends call in a favor, Sam is forced to face an entirely new line of duty—playing nanny for their newly divorced sister and her seven-month-old twins. Problem is, Sheridan has sworn off overbearing military men, so Sam must hide his identity. And that he's been ordered not to touch her. Ever. But even the most disciplined Marine has weaknesses...and Sheridan is one Sam might not be able to resist.

FIANCÉE FOR HIRE

Former Marine MacArthur Patton is used to handling top-secret government contracts and black-ops missions, but his new assignment involves something more dangerous—marriage. Enter his little sister's best friend Kelli Landers. She can't wait to bring Mr. Tall-Dark-and-Detached to his knees, and her longtime crush on the commitment-phobe makes her plan to seduce him even sweeter. Love wasn't part of the plan, but soon Mac and Kelli find that more than a weapons deal is on the line...

Other books by Tawna Fenske

EAT, PLAY, LUST